Why was she stonewalling? What did she know about that night that she wasn't telling him?

"The past is the past, I live with it every day. I want you to stop him in the here and now, before he tries to follow through on his threat. Just tell me you're here to help me."

There it was again, her palm pressed against the fabric in front of him.

J.P. stepped closer.

Eve Brooks was his client. All she wanted was his assurance he could help her, and protect her and catch the disgruntled kidnapper tormenting her. It was what he'd been hired to do.

Raising his hand, he put his palm to hers, reaffirming the existence of a physical connection emanating from their single point of contact.

"I'm here to help you, Eve, but you have to be honest with me. No detail is too small if it helps me catch him."

"I understand." Eve lowered her hand, slower this time, and J.P. thought she was about to tell him what he needed to know.

Instead, she said, "If there's nothing else, you know your way out."

JAN HAMBRIGHT

BRIDAL FALLS RANCH RANSOM

The heart knows what the mind and body resist.

That true beauty comes from deep within the soul.

Recycling programs for this product may not exist in your area.

ISBN-13: 978-0-373-69667-3

BRIDAL FALLS RANCH RANSOM

Copyright © 2013 by M. Jan Hambright

ABOUT THE AUTHOR

Jan Hambright penned her first novel at seventeen, but claims it was pure rubbish. However, it did open the door on her love for storytelling. Born in Idaho, she resides there with her husband, three of their five children, a three-legged watchdog and a spoiled horse named Texas, who always has time to listen to her next story idea while they gallop along.

A self-described adrenaline junkie, Jan spent ten years as a volunteer EMT in rural Idaho, and jumped out of an airplane at ten thousand feet attached to a man with a parachute, just to celebrate turning forty. Now she hopes to make your adrenaline level rise along with that of her danger-seeking characters. She would like to hear from her readers and hopes you enjoy the story world she has created for you. Jan can be reached at P.O. Box 2537, McCall, Idaho 83638.

Books by Jan Hambright

CAST OF CHARACTERS

J.P. Ryker—A former FBI agent, J.P. worked tactical operations for the FBI's hostage rescue unit, until a hostage was murdered before he could get to her. He quit the bureau and started his own security agency. He's doing fine until he takes Eve Brooks's case in Idaho and discovers an unresolved link to his past.

Eve Brooks—She's running scared after a botched ransom drop in the California desert and a horrible explosion that left her physically scarred. Hiding out at the Bridal Falls Ranch in Idaho seems to be the only hope she has of avoiding the disgruntled kidnapper who has contacted her again. That is, until she hires J.P. Ryker to protect her.

Thomas Avery—He's Eve's business partner in L.A. and the ex-fiancé who deserted her after the accident. He's an undisputed cad, but do his character flaws run deeper?

Edith Weber—Maybe the best personal assistant Eve has ever had.

Devon Hall—He's the foreman of the Bridal Falls Ranch.

Tyler Spangler—He's a member of the ranch crew who can ride and wrangle cattle, but does he have ambitions that go beyond being a cowpoke forever?

Roger Grimes—Eve's father bought up most of Roger's ranch before he died four years earlier. Has Roger discovered a way to get it back?

Jacqueline Cordova—What's her connection to the past?

Shelly McGinnis—Eve Brooks's half sister has been dead for three years thanks to a kidnapping gone wrong.

Chapter One

The kidnapper's call was seven minutes late.

Eve Brooks glanced at her Rolex in the glare of her headlights for the third time in less than ten minutes.

She pulled a deep breath into her lungs and tried to remain calm. She'd parked at the precise angle the kidnapper had requested, followed his every instruction in the ransom note she'd found under her wiper blade the same day he'd been taken. So why hadn't he called yet?

Frustrated, she shoved her hands into her coat pockets. Nervous tension turned to moisture on her palms as she clenched and unclenched her fists.

"He'll call," she whispered.

If he wants the ransom money, he'll call.

Cool night air seeped through her coat and raised chill bumps on her skin. She shivered, caught up in the involuntary response that quickly turned to speculation.

Maybe Thomas was already dead? Murdered by the brazen kidnapper who'd taken him at gunpoint from the parking garage in full view of a security camera?

A low mechanical stutter dragged her gaze to the west. She heard a rumble she recognized as air brakes on a big rig. Welcoming the distraction, she stared at its two pinpricks of light in the distance, watching the semi crest a shallow rise in the endless ribbon of asphalt she'd used to find this godforsaken rest stop in the desert above Los Angeles—

The rasp of the telephone ringing cut through her thoughts.

In one heart-stopping motion she yanked the pay phone's receiver from its cradle before it could ring a second time and pulled it to her ear.

"Yes. I'm here."

"Listen carefully. I'm only going to say this once." The kidnapper's disguised voice modulated over the phone connection. "Leave the receiver off the hook. Take the money and walk straight out into the desert. Stay in between your headlight beams. Fifty paces out you'll find a hole. Put the case in the hole and cover it with the dirt piled beside it. Come back and I'll tell you where to find him."

Dragging in an uneven breath, she willed a measure of courage into her bloodstream and straightened her spine.

"How do I know he's still alive? I want proof."

Dead airspace stretched between her and the man who'd kidnapped her business partner and soon-to-be husband, Thomas Avery, three days ago.

"Fair enough." Commotion crackled at the other end of the line, sending anticipation through her body in waves.

"Eve—"

"Thomas! Thomas, are you—"

"He's still breathing." The man's voice boomed over the connection, barely drowning out a thud in the background. Had he landed something against the side of Thomas's head to shut him up so he could reclaim the phone?

"Don't hurt him!"

"Shut up and bury the damn money!"

Like a robot operating on a battery charge of fear, she released the handset and felt a tug on her left earlobe as the receiver dropped.

A falling glimmer of gold caught in her car lights for a second before disappearing into the darkness on the ground at her feet.

Desperation needled her nerves and threatened to undo her composure. It was her earring. A gift from Thomas the day he'd proposed.

She stared down at the pea gravel but couldn't pick out the golden hoop. She'd have to find it later, after she'd followed the kidnapper's instructions. After he told her where to find Thomas. Nothing else mattered.

She turned and hurried to her car, opened the driver's side door and pressed the trunk release. It would all be over soon. Thomas would be freed. They could go back to their life together. The wedding was less than a month away. She hadn't even gotten the chance to tell him the Paris account he'd worked so hard to broker had come through the day he was taken. Her bridal gown collection would be strutted on fashion runways worldwide, thanks to him.

Emotion squeezed her throat shut as she fumbled for the case. She would give him the good news when she had him back.

Her fingers trembled as she wrapped them around the handle. She pulled the stainless steel briefcase from the trunk and closed the lid.

Half a million dollars in unmarked bills. It seemed like a pittance for a life. She couldn't screw this up. She knew full well the consequences if she didn't do exactly as she was told.

People died.

People you love died. But not this time. She'd done everything right. No cops. No questions. No witnesses. Just what he'd asked her to do.

Her doubts vanished as she made her way out into the

desert, walking in a straight line, relying on the glare of the headlights to hold back the darkness and keep her on track.

The soil under her feet was soft and sandy, swallowing her steps as she moved deep into the night. The tangy scent of damp sagebrush clung to the air, but it offered little in the way of comfort.

A blue-tailed lizard darted from a clump of dry grass and scurried across the path in front of her.

Her heart jolted in her chest, drumming against her rib cage, but she fought the urge to jump back. Instead she kept moving, kept pushing forward, counting off the paces stride by stride, pounding down her fear with the beat of each number in her head.

At forty-eight she stopped.

Searching the ground two feet in front of her she saw a black hole carved out in the desert floor just where he said it would be.

Caution pricked her brain, leaving her thoughts to bleed out unchecked. This could end like her half sister Shelly's kidnapping had. In murder, obscured by a trail of unanswered questions.

Eve pulled her shoulders back and gained a measure of certainty as she stared out across the desert landscape. Was he watching from somewhere out there? Gauging her level of commitment through a set of night-vision glasses, or goggles or whatever they were called?

Well, she wasn't going to disappoint him. She wanted Thomas back. Alive.

Stepping forward, she went to her knees, put the briefcase on the ground next to the hole and shoved it in.

It clunked against the earthen bottom a couple of feet down. Using her hands, she pushed the gritty soil in, listening to it patter against the rigid case like hard rain. In a matter of minutes she'd filled the hole and smoothed the last mound of dirt over the top. She scrambled to her feet, dusted off her hands and hurried back to the phone.

Clutching the receiver, she raised it to her ear. "I buried the money like you asked. Now, where's Thomas?"

"Directions to his location are taped to the bottom of the call box." A click at the end of the line was chased by a dial tone.

Eve's heart skipped a beat as she hung up the handset and slid her open hand, palm side up, into the narrow crevice between the telephone and the metal deck underneath it.

Feeling with her fingertips, she located a piece of paper. Crushing it against her palm with her thumb, she pulled it out.

Tension locked on every nerve ending in her body as she fumbled to open the folded note. Tipping it toward the headlights, she made out the address at the heart of the crude map. 16800 Pacific Coast Highway. Storm drain two...

A glitter of gold on the ground caught her attention. Her earring? She'd almost forgotten about it.

Fisting her hand around the map so it wouldn't dissolve, she took a step forward and squatted down to pick up the hoop from its spot in the loose gravel.

The semi she'd spotted miles out was on top of her now, vibrating the earth under her feet. Headlight beams flicked across her as the truck rumbled past on the highway a stone's throw away.

"Gotcha." Eve hooked the earring with her right index finger and started to straighten.

The ear-splitting squeal of rupturing metal penetrated her awareness.

Time slowed as a brilliant flash of fire stabbed toward

her on the left, sheathed in a deafening roar. Her teeth rattled in her head.

The ferocity of the blast hit her full force.

Percussion sent her skidding across the gravel like a tumbleweed. Her head slammed into the ground with a sickening thud that resonated to her toes.

Pain burned along the left side of her neck and across the top of her shoulder in hot trails of molten heat.

Stunned, she gasped for breath, her lungs on fire with the stench of her own singed flesh. Panic dragged her over the edge into an abyss. Darkness folded around her. She blinked, trying to focus her vision.

A copper-penny flavor bubbled inside her mouth. *Blood?* She closed her eyes, struggling to make sense of the last few seconds.

An explosion. From the telephone call box?

Realization gripped her mind as she digressed into a seizure. She succumbed to the convulsion.

There was no fighting the involuntary earthquake ripping through her muscles.

The squeal of truck tires locking up on asphalt penetrated the ringing in her eardrums.

Hope flooded her senses. She wouldn't die alone tonight. The semi's driver would stop.

The seizure dissipated.

Going with it, she relaxed into the dust and drifted down into unconsciousness, acutely aware of the golden hoop hooked on the index finger of her right hand and the map crushed in her fist.

Who would save Thomas now?

Chapter Two

Eight months later....

J.P. Ryker stared at the west-central Idaho landscape from the helicopter window and followed the direction of pilot Henry Brashear's finger point.

"There it is," he said, his voice coming in loud and clear over the bulky headset J.P. wore to drown out the drone of the rotor blades.

"The Bridal Falls Ranch. Homesteaded in 1890 by Miss Brooks's great-grandparents, Parnell and Evelyn Brooks."

"Frilly name for such a rugged place," he said into the mouthpiece as he sized the mountain peaks jousting for the sky.

"It's named after the landmark Evelyn Brooks discovered."

"A waterfall?"

"Yes." He let out an audible breath. "The prettiest veil of water on the entire mountain, according to every hardy Brooks woman who has ever horse-backed in for a look. There wasn't a Brooks man willing to argue the observation."

"So the name stuck?"

"Yeah."

The pilot squeezed the aircraft through a gap between

two epic mountains and dropped a thousand feet in elevation.

"How often do you fly in?"

"Twice a month, but I'm on permanent standby at the airport hangar in town whenever Miss Brooks requires my services."

Eve Brooks, one of those hardy Brooks women the pilot had spoken of, was his newest client. Too bad he didn't know any more about her situation now than he had a week ago when she'd contacted his L.A. security firm on a referral from a former client.

Only a face-to-face meeting with her was going to answer the myriad of questions he had and fatten the nearly empty case file tucked in his duffel bag.

It was a sorry start to an investigation: several publicity photos he'd pulled off the internet of the drop-dead gorgeous former model turned wedding gown designer to the stars, who dropped from sight six months ago like a stone in a pond, and a hard copy of a brief press release from her PR rep, stating that Eve had been injured in a minor accident and would be recovering at an undisclosed location. Hell, that could amount to a broken fingernail, based on the lack of specific detail in the release. But he had a hunch it had more to do with her admission to him that she'd been targeted by a kidnapper.

"Any other routes into this place?" he asked, studying the ranch's layout deep in the valley below, surrounded by pastures of lush green grass and a sentry of mountains that peaked just below a layer of high, thin clouds brushing across the open sky.

"Four-wheel drive if you take the road to Yellow Pine. It's rough, but doable unless we get a heavy thunderstorm. The highway in the other direction toward Cascade is paved but as twisted as a lasso on a steer."

J.P. gritted his teeth and focused on the sprawling ranch below, taking a degree of comfort in its remote location. Isolation could give him the upper hand when it came to protecting Eve Brooks.

"How long have you worked for her?"

"Almost six months, but I was on staff here before her father died four years ago. I have to admit, it feels good to be working for a Brooks again."

He glanced over at the smile of satisfaction on the pilot's face. *In the saddle again* crossed his mind when he thought of the passel of cowboy clothes zipped up in his duffel bag. He was going in undercover as the newest hire on the working cattle ranch. Eve Brooks needed a bodyguard and someone to investigate the threats being made against her.

"What do you think of Miss Brooks? How is she to talk to? Work for?" He cast a sideways glance at the man behind the controls of the chopper and watched his grin fade.

"I don't know. I haven't had a real conversation with Miss Brooks since her daddy's funeral." The pilot started his approach, aiming for a square of concrete west of a two-story log lodge and a massive barn painted in a shade of brick red. "Nobody but her personal assistant, Edith, gets face time with her. She's effectively closed herself off from everyone, including me."

"Why?"

"I'm not sure, but rumor has it, she was in some sort of accident. But her need for isolation just doesn't make any sense to me. She's a sweet woman, a pretty little thing too, with a smile that could make the sun rise early. I always enjoyed her and her family. Bottom line, son, you'll have to ask her yourself."

The pilot eased the helicopter down onto the landing pad.

"Good luck," Henry said into his mouthpiece.

J.P. nodded, shed his headset and shook the man's hand.

He grabbed his duffel bag from the floor in front of his seat and climbed out of the aircraft.

From the edge of the landing site he slapped a hand on his Stetson and watched the chopper lift off, gain altitude, hover for a moment and head off in the direction they'd come.

The sensation of being watched walked across the back of his neck before the dust from the rotors had time to settle. Turning, he stared at the lodge from underneath the brim of his hat and caught a flicker of movement in the frame of an upstairs window, seeing the blinds snap shut.

The mysterious Eve Brooks?

"J.P. Ryker?"

He glanced sideways at the man who approached him with an outstretched hand. "Yes, sir." He shook the man's hand.

"Devon Hall, ranch foreman. Miss Brooks said Henry would be flying you in this morning."

"Did she tell you why I'm here?"

Devon Hall pulled off his hat and whacked it against his jeans-clad thigh a couple of times, beating a puff of dust out of it before he set it back on his head.

"Yeah. I've kept my mouth shut around the crew in case one of them is involved, but they're a heck of a good bunch of men, Mr. Ryker. In my opinion, she's barking up the wrong tree."

"Has she said as much to you?"

"No. But this is a quiet place. The hardworking folks around here are salt of the earth. They mind their own business and help their neighbors. If anyone is causing trouble, they'd be the first to call him out."

Devon Hall. Friend or foe, he didn't know, but everyone on the Bridal Falls Ranch was suspect until he knew better.

"Thanks for the heads-up."

"Miss Brooks is waiting for you over in the main lodge. After you visit, come on up to the ranch office." Devon pointed to a row of low-slung buildings shaded in a cluster of pine trees a hundred yards due west.

"I'll get you settled in one of the private bunkhouse rooms with Wi-Fi and a landline. Did you bring a laptop?"

"Yeah."

"Good." Devon studied him for a moment then frowned. "I'm gonna need that hat."

"My hat?" It was a strange request.

"It's got city all over it, but I've got a remedy."

Reaching up, he took off the black Stetson that had set him back two hundred bucks and handed it to the ranch foreman. "Keep it clean, will ya?"

The foreman tucked his chin, but not before he saw a hint of a smirk on the man's sun-baked face. It quickly vanished under the slope of his hat brim.

"Better get moving. Miss Brooks knows you're here and she doesn't like to wait." Devon walked away.

He watched the foreman head straight for a corral of nervous horses, probably still riled up by the helicopter's descent on their peaceful May morning.

Turning, he aimed for the lodge. Did he really have city written all over him? He'd been raised in a small town and ridden his share of horses before he'd relocated to Los Angeles just out of college and Quantico, where he'd worked for the FBI's hostage tactical unit up until he'd resigned two years ago.

Yeah, maybe he did have city all over him, but he wasn't sure how giving his hat to the foreman of the ranch was going to remedy that.

The slap of a screen door brought his chin up. He studied the woman standing on the porch in front of him.

"Mr. Ryker, I'm Edith Weber, Miss Brooks's personal assistant. If you'll come with me, I'll take you up to speak with her."

"Thanks." He followed the middle-aged woman through the open door and let the screen pop shut behind him.

"You can leave your bag next to the door if you like."

He paused in the entrance long enough to scope out the inside of the lodge and put his duffel bag down.

"The ranch hands and staff take their meals in the dining room." She motioned to a massive table surrounded by a dozen high-backed chairs.

"Breakfast is served at seven a.m., lunch at noon unless the crew is out working cattle, and dinner is at six p.m. on the dot. The washrooms are just inside the back door where we came in. Miss Brooks expects everyone to be clean and respectful."

"Miss Brooks runs a tight ship."

"Yes, she does." Edith turned away from him and headed for a closed door to the left of the living room, dominated by a massive river-rock fireplace.

"Does Miss Brooks take her meals with the crew?"

Edith's steps faltered slightly, a brief hesitation the average observer would have missed, but he homed in on it, watching the woman's shoulders stiffen and her head droop forward for a moment.

"No, sir. Miss Brooks takes her meals upstairs."

Curiosity scraped across his nerves, but he planned to save his questions for Eve Brooks. That restraint nearly fizzled when Edith put a skeleton key in the lock of the door and turned it.

"You keep her locked up?"

"It's not to keep her in, Mr. Ryker. It's to keep others out."

J.P. gritted his teeth, more determined than before to

find out what was going on. He knew Eve Brooks wasn't a monster. He'd spoken with her on the phone. In fact, he still hadn't been able to get the sweet sound of her voice out of his head. But finding her sequestered like a beauty locked in a tower? He didn't know what to think; he only knew he didn't believe in fairy tales.

Edith pulled the door open and stepped back. "She's waiting for you. Go into the first room on the right at the top of the stairway. There's a chair next to the screened wall. Have a seat. She'll speak with you there."

He searched the woman's face for a clue to her emotions, but she gave him a bland smile and closed the door behind him.

The clatter of the key in the lock heightened his level of caution and pushed him up the stairs two at a time until he reached the landing.

What sort of freak show were they headlining at Bridal Falls Ranch? he wondered.

But it didn't matter. He already had a ticket....

EVE RUBBED HER BARE arms with her hands, trying to dispel the tension buzzing in every one of her nerve endings, but the sound of J.P. Ryker's boots against the hardwood floor only compounded the problem.

She'd watched him climb out of the chopper, wishing her friend Tina Davis, who'd used his agency's services as a bodyguard once, had bothered to forewarn her. The last thing she needed on the ranch was a six-foot-plus, lethal male looker working her case, but that's exactly what she had, and like it or not, he was here now.

The door hinges squawked. Eve froze in her tracks behind the screen wall. She pulled in a deep calming breath, then another, just as her therapist had taught her to do, until she felt the effect take control of her mind and body.

It didn't matter how good-looking Ryker was. She'd been pursued by dozens of men better looking than him. He was here to protect her and stop the kidnapper who'd reentered her life. Nothing more, nothing less.

She swallowed hard and took a step forward, trying to gauge his location in the adjacent room.

"Mr. Ryker, I'm Eve Brooks. Welcome to Bridal Falls Ranch. I trust you had a good trip?"

J.P. stared at the nonrigid wall separating him from the same sweet voice he'd heard over the phone line less than a week ago. "Yes, I did." He leaned closer, working to pick up her movements through the dense fabric stretched taut between them.

"If it will help, I'll turn on the backlight."

The click of a switch instantly filled the room she was in with illumination.

He stepped back, staring at the silhouette outlined against the fabric. "Damn."

"Speculate if you like. I have my reasons, but I didn't hire you to question my need for absolute privacy."

J.P. listened to her as he traced her curves with his gaze.

"I hired you because the kidnapper who took my fiancé, Thomas Avery, has resurfaced."

"Did he collect the original ransom?"

"No." Her voice broke. "He left my half a million dollars right where he told me to bury it in the California desert. The local sheriff dug it up a week later and returned it to me in the hospital."

"And you believe the kidnapper intends to try and collect it now?"

"Yes."

"Did Mr. Avery survive his ordeal?"

"He was found, barely alive, chained in a storm drain

along the Pacific Coast Highway. Another day and he wouldn't have survived."

"Who compromised the money drop?" he asked, listening to her sharp intake of breath. He watched her turn slightly and bow her head.

Concern overrode his senses and roped his emotions, gathering them in a tight knot. He knew what she was feeling; he'd been in the same spot dozens of times.

"You believe you did?"

"I know I did," she whispered.

"Guilt is a lethal adversary. It'll eat you alive. Take it from me, kidnapping situations can spin out of control in a heartbeat. It's no one's fault—"

"Spare me the psychobabble, Mr. Ryker. I get that from my therapist. I want you to catch the bastard."

He sobered, watching her turn and move up next to the screen less than a foot from where he stood. The impression of her palm pressing against the fabric wall surprised him.

Instinctively he reached out to her, melding his open hand to hers.

Heat passed between them. A spark he couldn't explain, or deny. "I'll do everything in my power to stop him, but I need to know the details."

She pulled her hand back as if the contact suddenly burned. "I've received two phone calls from him here at the ranch."

"I'll put a wiretap on your landline. If he calls again we can record him."

Her feet shuffled against the floor on the other side. He watched her shadow ripple back and forth across the screen.

"Three weeks ago, I got the first call. He demanded that

I bring the money to L.A. and leave it in the same damn hole in the desert. I told him to go to hell and hung up."

He grinned, glad she couldn't see him. The woman had spunk, he'd give her that. "Did you recognize his voice when he called here? Was he the same man you spoke with the first time around?"

"I can't be certain."

"What do you mean?"

"His voice was altered."

"So you believe he used a device to disguise it?"

"Yeah, I guess he must have."

"Those gadgets are a dime a dozen on the internet. For sixty bucks you can sound like Mickey Mouse if you want to."

Concern looped around him. It was common practice for an intelligent kidnapper to alter his voice in order to forgo the risk of identification through voice recognition if he was eventually caught and prosecuted.

"What about his second call?"

"Same voice, but my assistant, Edith, took the call while I listened in. He wants the money brought to the same location, and this time he threatened to hurt me. Cut me up, he said, if I don't give him the money in the next two weeks. He claimed he'd come to the ranch and make my life miserable until I pay."

"You didn't call the authorities or the FBI?"

"No. I don't trust them...." Her voice faltered, its lilt hinting at a measure of regret. "I didn't trust them to get Thomas back alive then, and I don't trust them now."

He opened his mouth to defend his former employer, but shut it, remembering the number of times things had gone unpredictably bad on his watch.

"Why wasn't he able to collect the ransom the first time around?"

She stopped pacing, the hesitation piquing his interest. "An accident brought the local Kern County authorities to the location of the money drop. The kidnapper must have thought it was too risky to try and dig it up with cops everywhere, so he walked away. I'd already been given Thomas's location. The Malibu police found him right where the kidnapper's map said he would be."

"What sort of accident?"

"It's inconsequential. It had no bearing on the kidnapping."

Why was she stonewalling? What did she know about that night that she wasn't telling him?

"The past is the past. I live with it every day. I want you to stop him in the here and now, before he tries to follow through on his threat. Just tell me you're here to help me."

There it was again, her palm pressed against the fabric in front of him.

He stepped closer.

Eve Brooks was his client. All she wanted was his assurance he could help her, and protect her and catch the disgruntled kidnapper tormenting her. It was what he'd been hired to do.

Raising his hand, he put his palm to hers, reaffirming the existence of a physical connection emanating from their single point of contact.

"I'm here to help you, Eve, but you have to be honest with me. No detail is too small if it helps me catch him."

"I understand." Eve lowered her hand, slower this time, determined to control the heated attraction gliding over her senses.

"There's an extra skeleton key hanging next to the door at the bottom of the stairs. Take it. We'll talk again tomorrow morning and you can have access to the lodge's telephone system so you can install your wiretap. If there's nothing else, you know your way out."

She listened to the steady beat of his cowboy boots on the hardwood floor and worked to slow her heartbeat. She didn't move until he was gone, resisting the urge to split the blinds with her fingertips and take another look at J.P. Ryker.

But some details were better left to her imagination. Besides, he'd take one look at her and run like hell.

Chapter Three

J.P. sat across from Devon Hall and tried not to stare at his desecrated cowboy hat lying like a limp head of lettuce on the desk between them. He could bet it'd been trampled at least once by every horse in the corral, judging by the number of dusty hoof marks all over it.

A lopsided grin pulled on the ranch foreman's mouth. "You fit in now. That hat was a dead giveaway. My crew would have been on to you faster than a rope on a runaway horse."

"I appreciate that." He nodded. "Glad you're looking out for me, but I want to pick my own mount or I'm likely to end up on last year's rodeo bronc."

Devon chuckled. "A sense of humor goes a long way out here, J.P."

He didn't doubt it. "I'll try to remember that."

"I have an employment file on each of the ranch hands I've hired, but no background checks. I suppose you'll want to take a look at them?"

"It could be helpful. See if anyone on the crew has something to hide."

Devon shoved a notepad and pen across the desk to him. "Give me your email address and I'll forward them this afternoon."

He scribbled the information on the paper, amazed technology had found the Bridal Falls Ranch and its foreman even in such an isolated area. The files would provide him with the stealth needed to investigate each member of the crew from his laptop. He put the pad back on the desk.

"Can I get my BlackBerry to work out here?"

Devon Hall chuckled. "In these parts, J.P., a BlackBerry is something you pick off a bush in late September and ask your momma to put in a pie."

"Understood. Duties?" he asked, snagging his crumpled hat off the desk and molding it back into shape with his hands.

"Miss Brooks wants you close to the main lodge, so you'll be here on the homestead."

"Won't the other ranch hands wonder why I'm not in the saddle?"

"Maybe, but I'll handle them. You've got a couple of weeks before they start asking questions."

"With any luck, I'll have this case wrapped up by then." He stared at Devon, wondering how much Eve had told him about being harassed by a kidnapper. "What exactly did Miss Brooks say I'd be doing on the ranch?"

"To the crew, you're another hired hand, but Miss Brooks told me you're here to find out who's stealing semen from our Brahman bull breeding program. It's used in artificial insemination and frozen in liquid nitrogen. Someone took a couple of cylinders three weeks ago. Our prize bull Dust-Up's genetic material is worth big bucks, and the Bridal Falls could take a substantial financial hit if his offspring show up somewhere else. Miss Brooks wants the culprit found ASAP."

He gritted his teeth and nodded. It was an interesting cover he'd never expected to be wearing. *Sperm theft investigator?*

"Could be in excess of a million dollars once the stolen lineage is established and the young bulls are used in their own breeding programs."

"Is there any way the culprit could be a threat to Miss Brooks's safety?"

"It's possible, if she were to catch him in the act. Don't know how he'd respond."

Devon's answer didn't sit well in the back of his mind. It added another level of threat to Eve's situation. Granted it probably wasn't as lethal as the kidnapper who'd already threatened to hurt her, but unpredictable nonetheless. He'd have to take it seriously.

"Come on, I'll get you lined out on your bunkhouse room."

He followed the foreman out of the office and paused at the distinctive drum of horse hooves striking hard-packed earth and the bellow of cows searching for their calves in the commotion. A pack of horsemen three deep and half a dozen strong wrangled a herd of cattle toward an open gate leading into a massive pasture thigh deep in grass.

"It's branding season. You're one of five temporary hires I've got coming in this week. We sure could use your help if Miss Brooks is okay with it."

"Just say the word. I've spent some time in the saddle."

He walked next to Devon Hall, picking out the small cabin he aimed for and analyzing its proximity to everything on the ranch. He'd have an unobstructed view of all the goings-on, the main lodge, the barn and Eve's upstairs window.

A charge pulsed through him, grounded by the image of her hand pressed against the screen, begging for hope only he could give her. He didn't know what her reasons were for hiding, but he intended to find out. Until then he would respect her need for anonymity, even if he found it crazy-odd.

"We'll need you when it comes time to cut the calves out of the herd and drive them into the holding pen. Their mamas get a little aggravated."

"No problem." He took the steps behind Devon onto the covered porch, listening to the creak of the wooden stairs under his boot soles. Only the second step offered up a sound. He backtracked onto it to make sure his observation was correct before he stepped onto the landing and walked through the door the foreman had already opened.

"It's a nice place. Should serve your needs."

He surveyed the interior of the cabin from the neatly made double bed to the adjoining bath. He put his duffel bag down on the bed. "It'll suffice."

Devon nodded. "Step outside. I'll point out the members of the crew."

He followed the foreman as he moseyed out onto the porch, where he locked his hands on the railing and pushed his hat back.

Stepping up next to Devon, he eyed the mounted riders pushing the last of the cattle through the gate into the pasture.

"The cowboy on the big bay horse is Tyler Spangler, been at Bridal Falls since before Hank Brooks died."

"Four years ago?" J.P. asked, clarifying the information he'd gleaned from Henry the chopper pilot.

"Yeah. He was foreman here before Miss Brooks took over the operation and put me in charge."

"How'd that sit with him, you taking his position?" The pointed question hung in the air between them like a dagger.

Devon's shoulders tensed but slowly relaxed as he turned toward him. "He was mad as hell. Probably still carrying a grudge, but there wasn't much he could do to me in a full leg cast. Tyler got busted up pretty bad that year at the Riggins' Rodeo. He wasn't in any position to argue with Miss Brooks."

He nodded and turned his attention back to the cowboys. "The man on the paint?"

"Buck Walters, the oldest member of the crew. Solid. Came to work here three years ago. Ruckus Bartlett on that damn leopard Appaloosa he insists on riding, he's been here for a year and a half. Dave Haney is on the palomino. Another solid guy, been here the same length of time as Buck."

"Three years?"

"Yeah. The last two pokes on the sorrel quarter horses are Cody and Troy Profit. Idaho cowboys, brothers, both former bull riders. Cody took the PRCA championship buckle in Vegas two years ago, and Troy came home in an ambulance."

"What happened?"

"Took a bull horn just below his flat-jacket after his qualifying ride. Messed up his insides, but he pulled through. Had to give up the circuit, but we're glad he's here."

"You're right, Devon. You've got a good crew." Every one of them fit the definition of a cowpoke. Hats, boots and a horse, but he planned to look past the obvious. Did any of them have a record?

The foreman pushed back from the railing. "Lunch is in half an hour. You'll know it when Charleen starts clanging the dinner bell down at the lodge." He took the steps and paused at the bottom. "I'll make proper introductions then."

"I'll be there." J.P. watched the foreman walk away before turning back into the cabin. There was a good mix of wranglers on the Bridal Falls Ranch, he didn't doubt it. But could one of them be responsible for kidnapping

Thomas Avery and threatening Eve Brooks over the un-claimed ransom money?

He wasn't sure, but he planned to check out each and every one of them as soon as Devon Hall sent him the employee files. In the meantime he'd get to know them at lunch. A handshake could tell a lot about a man. That and the look in his eyes.

A LACK OF NOISE BROUGHT J.P. up out of bed. Pushing back the covers, he sat up, getting his bearings in the unfamiliar room.

He'd always cussed the drone of traffic in the street below his apartment window in L.A. Now he'd give anything to be lulled to sleep by the revving of a hundred car engines.

It was just too quiet.

He stood up, went to the door, pulled it open and stepped out onto the narrow porch.

A fat yellow moon hung in the night sky almost directly overhead. He stared at the face of his watch in its glow and muffled a curse. Two a.m. Two blasted a.m. Shrugging it off, he pulled in a breath of cool mountain air, tinged with evergreen. He'd survived on less sleep before, and he could do it again.

Somewhere in the distance a whisper of a sound caught and held his attention.

Turning his head slightly, he tried to pick it up for a second time.

Clip-clop, clip-clop, clip-clop. The steady drum of shod hooves striking the earth, but it shouldn't surprise him. This was a ranch with lots of horses. Hoofbeats in the night were normal, but these seemed to be coming from north of the main pasture, somewhere along the road into the ranch.

Caution edged through him. He stepped back from the

railing, out of the glaring moonlight and into the shadows underneath the overhang.

Picking out the location of the sound, he watched a single mounted rider spurt out of the tree line to the north and maneuver his horse toward the barn. The hat on his head glowed an eerie white in the blaze of moonlight and blotted out the face of its wearer from under its brim.

He didn't know a single cowboy poke who herded cattle at night. Maybe the lone rider's presence signaled something more dangerous. Maybe he was here to steal more semen samples from the cryo room in the barn?

J.P. backed through the door at the same time the rider disappeared through the main doors into the barn. He slipped on his jeans, boots and a shirt. Feeling between the mattress and box spring, he pulled out his Glock.

If the thief stealing from Eve Brooks tried to escape, he'd pin him down at gunpoint and turn him over to the local sheriff's department.

Clipping the holster on his belt, he slipped outside, sticking to the shadows as he ducked from cover to cover, until he reached the barn and squeezed through a narrow opening in the massive doors at the back of the structure.

The rustle of livestock in their stalls went with the dusty smell of sawdust and hay. The interior of the barn was pitch-black and it took an instant for his eyes to adjust as he flattened himself against the wall next to the opening.

Scanning for movement, he picked up a flit of white near the front of the structure, near the insulated room where the stainless steel vat of frozen samples were kept.

He couldn't let the thug take what didn't belong to him.

Adrenaline pulsed in his veins. Moving away from the wall, he went straight for the tall thin figure now framed in the doorway and about to exit the barn on foot.

He lunged for the man and body slammed him from behind, sending them both through the barn door in a tangle of flailing arms and legs.

A feminine shriek grazed his eardrums and sucked his breath away even before they both hit the ground in a puddle of dust.

Terror crushed Eve in its grip. She came up fighting. Kicking and screaming, she lashed out at the man who pinned her to the ground beneath him.

"Get off of me!" she screamed, panic consuming her entire body. "Get off!"

"Eve? What are you doing out here?" He rolled away from her and pushed up onto his knees.

She scrambled to her feet, careful to keep her head bent forward. "I ride at night." She turned her back on him. "I don't appreciate being tackled. Don't do it again." She took off at a jog, leaving him behind in the dust.

Focused on the back door of the lodge, she didn't dare look over her shoulder for fear he'd take it as an invitation to follow. But there were no footsteps behind her, no pursuit. She reached the house and hurried inside, gunning for the safety of her prison upstairs. She hadn't felt this overwhelmed since the night of the explosion. Since she'd lain in the gravel and felt her life slipping away.

Her chest tightened as she slotted the skeleton key in the lock, turned it and stepped inside. Hand shaking, she locked herself in, hung her key on its peg and sat down on the bottom step.

Pulling in one deep breath after another, she attempted to waylay the panic attack consuming her bit by bit.

"Control…control. I'm safe. No one is going to hurt me again," she whispered as she slowly ran her hands down her jean-clad legs clear to her toes, feeling the physical affirmation of her words.

She was safe. She was intact. She was alive.

The fear dissipated. Short-circuited by the technique her therapist had taught her, and the bottle of pills upstairs in her medicine cabinet.

She stood and turned, then headed up the stairs, still conscious of the imprint J.P. Ryker's body had left on hers. It was a pleasant sensation, and that fact bothered her the most.

J.P. FINGERED THE WHITE cowboy hat he'd retrieved from the dirt and fumbled with its strange appendage, a heavy veil attached to the brim. He'd never seen anything like it before. With the fabric down, it would completely obscure the wearer's face. But why would she want to hide hers? She was beautiful.

A light flicked on upstairs in the lodge. He dragged his gaze to the window and saw her move in front of the closed blind, once, twice, three times. The mysterious Eve Brooks had just multiplied her mystique in his estimation. Riding at night, wearing a hat with a veil. Staying sequestered in her upstairs room during the day and materializing at night. Was she nocturnal? Maybe.

He turned for the bunkhouse, determined to get some finite answers in the morning. The instant he pushed open the door and stepped into the cabin, he knew he wasn't alone.

He dropped the hat in his hand and reached for his weapon, but not fast enough.

Behind him, the shuffle of movement echoed in his eardrums. He tried to pivot, but something hard made contact with his skull. Pain pulsed through his head. His vision blurred.

Stumbling forward in the dark, he tried to compensate for the brutal impact, feeling a trickle of blood zigzag down the back of his neck.

Dazed, he spun around, prepared to charge the dark silhouette to the left of the open door.

"You SOB," he whispered, feeling the room gyrate around him.

He took a shaky step toward the intruder, determined to stop him, determined to discover his identity in the middle of the fracas.

His knees buckled.

He fought to stay on his feet, to maintain his stance, but it was hopeless. He stepped forward and fell, hitting the floor like a stone.

The world went black, but not before he heard the scuff of a single pair of boots against the hardwood floor.

His assailant was a cowboy. A cowboy who most likely rode for the Bridal Falls Ranch.

Chapter Four

J.P. came to with a shaft of sunlight knifing into his eyes through the open door. His body hurt as if a herd of wild mustangs had trampled him during the night. His head throbbed in unison with his galloping heartbeat.

He eased up into a sitting position and scanned the interior of the bunkhouse. The place had been ransacked, probably while he'd been hot on the trail of Eve Brooks last night, believing she was a thief about to raid the sperm bank. His right elbow brushed against his holster. Tension sliced across his nerves. He reached back to finger the holster still clipped to his belt. His Glock was gone.

Staring at the mattress, he crawled to the bed and slid his hand between it and the box spring.

In the gap his fingers came in contact with the spare pistol he'd brought along, a .41 Magnum. He dragged himself to his feet and willed away a wave of concern. The assailant had gotten the jump on him and used one big club on the back of his head. So why hadn't he finished him off when he had the chance?

"J.P. Buddy?" A long low whistle hissed from between Devon Hall's lips as the ranch foreman stepped into the room. "I got to wondering about you when you didn't show for breakfast. What the hell happened in here?"

Following Devon's line of sight, he stared at the desk,

where he'd set up a makeshift office. The contents of his files lay scattered on the floor, but it was his trashed laptop lying upside down that worried him the most. Someone had removed the hard drive and with it everything he knew about Eve Brooks and her case.

"Someone jumped me last night. They were looking for something. I'd guess they found it. Did you hear anything?" he asked as he ran his hand over the back of his head, fingering the blood-matted hair caked over a knot.

"I heard Miss Brooks ride out around one, but I don't recall hearing much after that, seeing as I was holding a royal flush in my hand and counting the entire crew's chips in my head."

"The whole crew was playing poker?"

"Yeah."

So every cowpoke on the ranch had an alibi along with their empty pockets, but he was more curious about Devon's revelation.

"Does Miss Brooks ride every night?" He conjured the image of her lanky body pressed against him in the darkness.

"Nope. Two or three times a week at the most. Some nights she just sits out on the front porch of the lodge in the dark. It's peculiar, but I just work for her and keep my mouth shut. I figure this here's her spread, she can do whatever she wants, whenever she wants."

"I'm going to need those employee files again, but in hard copy this time."

"No problem. I'll print them off this morning."

Unable to resist any longer, he eased himself down on the corner of the bed. "I'll be along shortly."

"It'll take a couple of hours for him to get here, but I can have Doc Morton drive out to take a look at you."

"I'll live."

Devon Hall took a couple of steps and paused on the threshold between the room and the porch. "Charlene saved you some breakfast."

"Thanks. I'll be there after I get cleaned up." He watched the ranch foreman take the steps and turn to the right, probably headed for his office. His stare fell on the white, veil-draped hat lying on the floor next to the door.

Pushing up from the edge of the bed, he stepped to the door and pushed it closed. Something was going on, and apparently Eve wasn't the only one in danger once he started digging around at the Bridal Falls Ranch.

Reaching down, he scooped up the white hat from the floor. He needed to know what sort of accident had botched the money drop in California, and if Eve Brooks's odd behavior was tied to the answer.

EVE STARED THROUGH a narrow opening in the blinds, watching J.P. Ryker's deliberate strides toward the lodge. There was no doubt in her mind, judging by the determined way he carried himself, he was on a mission.

He was going to want specifics from her that she'd yet to give him. That fact and the sight of her white hat grasped in his hand warned of an impending showdown.

She swallowed the lump forming in her throat and pushed back against the rise of nerves pricking her insides. With a simple wave of her hand, she'd been able to avoid the hard questions. That and the amount of money she'd spent to disappear, to dig her way underground and as far away from the world she'd known as she could possibly get, without being six feet under. But that approach wasn't going to work with him.

Reaching up, she touched the left side of her face with her hand and willed her trembling fingers to still on the swath of skin grafts that started on her cheekbone and ran all the way down the side of her neck and across the top of her shoulder.

She hadn't come to grips with this yet, and she didn't expect anyone else to either. So when J.P. arrived to question her, she'd ask him to leave. To go back to Los Angeles and forget he'd ever agreed to take her case. She would find another bodyguard to help her. Someone who didn't need every gritty detail.

Letting the shade snap shut, she turned for her room behind the screen. Could she let the kidnapper come after her? If so, she hoped he'd kill her quickly when she refused to give him the money. It couldn't be any worse than the slow death she was living now.

J.P. SLOWED HIS MARCH, watching a white cargo van pull into the ranch driveway and roll to a stop. High-Country Delivery was painted on the driver's side door in bold black letters. The company logo of snow-capped mountains peaked just under the banner.

The driver climbed out, went around to the back of the van, opened the cargo doors and retrieved a package. Glancing up he spotted J.P. from under the brim of his ball cap with the same company logo stitched across the bill.

"Good morning," he said, juggling his clipboard and the plain brown cardboard box. "I've got a parcel for Eve Brooks."

"I'm headed in to speak with her right now. I'll take it."

"Sign here." He handed J.P. the clipboard.

He scribbled his signature and exchanged the clipboard for the parcel. "Thanks."

The man nodded and climbed back into his vehicle, fired the engine and pulled around the circle drive.

Stowing the box under his arm, he continued toward the lodge, mulling the questions he had for Eve.

The pop of the screen door brought his head up.

Edith Weber came down the steps. "Mr. Ryker, thanks for signing for that."

"No problem." He handed it off to her and fell in behind her as she went inside the lodge.

"Miss Brooks is waiting for you upstairs. I'll take her hat." She gestured to it.

"If you don't mind, I'd like to keep it."

She nodded, but the color vanished from her cheeks before she turned for the kitchen with the box in hand. What did she know that he didn't? Frustration tightened the muscles between his shoulder blades as he pivoted and headed for the door leading upstairs.

Pulling the skeleton key out of his pocket, he fit it into the lock. In a matter of minutes he was up the stairs and stepping into the partitioned room. Only then did he allow anticipation to seep out into his bloodstream.

"Eve. Are you here?"

"Yes."

"I've got your hat. I found it after our encounter last night in the barn. I'd like to give it back to you." He rolled the brim with his fingertips.

"You can leave it in the room." Her tone was flat, matter-of-fact, but he focused on the slightest hint of regret, as if she'd somehow given up.

"You should have told me you like to ride at night. Next time I won't run you down thinking you're a thug."

"There isn't going to be a next time, J.P."

He focused on the screen, trying to pick out her place in the room behind it, but she stood perfectly still. Stepping forward he got closer, close enough to hear her pull in a long inhale and let it out slowly.

"I've decided I can handle this myself—"

"If you think being sequestered in this room behind a

damn curtain is going to keep him from getting to you, you're fooling yourself. If he can't physically touch you here, he'll touch someone you love with as much brutality as he can unleash."

An earthquake of emotion rocked Eve's insides and penetrated her thoughts like a bullet through a target. She knew he was right. Knew it without having to analyze it. What if this stranger went after Thomas again? Or her mother? Or her stepfather, Simon? Hadn't they already suffered enough living through Shelly's kidnapping and murder, finding her lifeless body dumped outside the gate of their estate like a bag of garbage?

Hot tears singed the back of her eyelids. She blinked them away, feeling the first tick of a panic attack zing across her chest. She pulled in a deep breath and let it out. Then another.

"I'm sorry to be so blunt with you. I just want you to know what you could be letting yourself in for."

Closing her eyes, she mentally took cover behind her lids. J.P. was right. She'd be an idiot to think she could take on this maniac all by herself. She needed him now more than ever.

"Come back in an hour." She had to hide for a while, reconstitute her grit. Then she'd go toe-to-toe with him to come up with a strategy. Something that never involved him seeing her face, or what was left of it.

She opened her eyes and focused on the screen between them. "Then we'll put together a plan of action. Hire more security to stand guard 24/7 if necessary."

"It's too late for that," he whispered.

Fear skidded across her nerve endings, leaving them raw. "You believe he's already here?"

"While I was following your movements last night thinking you might be a thief or the kidnapper, someone ransacked my room, stole the hard drive out of my laptop, knocked me unconscious and stole the Glock from my holster."

Panic tightened her throat. "Someone on my crew?"

"I know for sure he was wearing cowboy boots. Devon emailed me the employee files on every man in the crew. That information took a hike along with my hard drive. He could be trying to cover up his background information. I'll have to go over the files in hard copy and run my investigation over the landline."

"I have a computer in my studio. If it'll expedite the process, you're welcome to use it."

"Eve?" The sound of Edith's voice echoed up the stairwell, followed by her solid footsteps on the wood. "You have a package, dear…could be in regards to Amanda Blackburn's wedding gown. I know you've been waiting for it to arrive from L.A. I haven't opened the box yet—" Edith stopped at the top of the stairs and glanced sideways, making eye contact with him.

J.P. sobered, irritated by the interrupted progress he felt he was making with Eve.

"Oh. Excuse me, Mr. Ryker. I thought you'd already left." Her gaze settled on the hat he still held in his hand before lifting to his face.

"I'll just go into the studio and open this for Miss Brooks." She indicated the parcel in her hand, then turned for the door at the end of the hallway.

J.P. stared after her, getting a quick view of the studio just before she closed the door behind her.

"I might take you up on your offer to use the computer, but first we have to come to an understanding." He waited for a reply, less than satisfied when she didn't immediately speak.

"You want to know why I was wearing that hat last night, don't you?"

"I want to know why you think you have to wear it. Why you hide up here and what in the hell it has to do, if anything, with the botched money drop? Because it all seems to start there." If he listened close enough, he swore he could hear her heartbeat amp up. "What happened to you, Eve?"

A soft moan whispered through the fabric separating them, making him want to retract the question, but he stood firm. He was determined to coax every detail out of her. Overlooked details could get them both killed.

She was on the move now, her footsteps scuffing against the floor, tracing a back-and-forth pattern behind the screen. Why was this so difficult for her? Guilt? Maybe. Outrage that Thomas almost lost his life because of some perceived mistake she'd made?

If so, what was it?

"I almost died that night," she whispered, pulling in an audible breath as if she were trying to suck in courage along with oxygen.

"If a semi hadn't been driving past the drop site when the pipe bomb went off…I would have bled out on the side of the highway."

"The kidnapper tried to kill you with an explosion?" Frustration hissed through J.P.'s veins, tempting him to rip down the wall separating them so he could take her in his arms.

"No. I was simply in the right place at the wrong time. It wasn't the first time a bomb had been planted at that remote call box."

"How bad?" he asked, remembering a segment from his FBI training dealing with blast injuries.

"Three weeks in ICU. Another month with my jaw

wired shut, rehabilitation on my left shoulder and plastic surgery on my…" Her words trailed off, leaving him hanging.

Face?

"The county sheriff was able to connect the blast that injured me to four others in a countywide area linked to some anarchist student group."

"I'm sorry, Eve. I had no idea."

"No one does. My PR rep was able to keep the worst of my medical information out of the press, and I plan to keep it that way."

Anger boiled up inside of him. He wanted the bastards who'd placed the pipe bomb now, almost as much as he wanted the kidnapper who'd picked the location for the money drop. Right now, he had neither. There was only the woman on the other side of the screen who needed his protection.

"We'll stop him this time, Eve." Reaching out, he pressed his open hand against the fabric. "I promise."

Heat arched between them even before he felt her palm meet his. "Maybe the thug who clocked me last night wasn't the kidnapper. Maybe he was trying to find out if I had information about the missing cryogenic cylinders. He could be behind the bull semen thefts Devon told me about."

The uncoupling of their palms was accompanied by the trill of nervous laughter. "I'm sorry," she said. "I should have told you. I took the cylinders before I hired you. I needed a seemingly legitimate reason to bring you on board in a policing capacity that Devon would believe. No one on the ranch except Edith knows about Thomas's kidnapping, how I was injured or that the kidnapper has made contact with me again."

The humor in the ruse found its mark and made him

grin. "So I don't have to list sperm cop on any future job refer—"

A metallic clatter blended with a high-pitched scream and resonated through the upstairs rooms.

The hairs on the back of J.P.'s neck came to attention.

"It's Edith," Eve yelled. "Something's wrong!"

Tossing Eve's hat into the corner, he bolted for the closed door at the end of the hallway.

Grasping the knob, he turned it and slipped into the room, where Edith Weber stood with one hand pressed against her chest. Wide-eyed, she pointed a shaky finger at the box on the edge of the table. Taking a step back, she shuddered, shook her head and covered her mouth with her hand.

In four steps he reached the work space. Eve's work space, judging by the sheets of delicate line drawings depicting wedding dresses. But the beautiful images warred with the repulsive smell invading his nostrils. Rotting flesh, distinct in its putrid stench.

J.P. lifted his arm and pressed his nose into the crux at his elbow.

Reaching down, he pulled back the solid-black plastic sheeting Edith had cut through, probably with the scissors on the floor right where she'd dropped them.

Staring at the carnage, he gritted his teeth.

A rat the size of his fist lay splayed in the box. Neatly gutted, cut up into pieces, packaged and sent to Eve Brooks.

Cut up. The exact words the kidnapper had used when he'd threatened Eve in his second phone call.

J.P. sobered as he lapped the flaps of the box.

"I need a paper sack, Edith, and a plastic bag, something I can seal this in."

"I'll get someone to take it to the trash can outside."

"I'm not going to toss it."

Her eyes went wide for an instant before a look of horror twisted her features. "You're going to keep it!"

"I'm going to send it out for forensic analysis. Maybe we'll get lucky and find out who sent it to Miss Brooks. I'm going to need a box to ship it in, too."

Edith exited the studio and J.P. listened to her hurried footfalls on the stairs. In less than half a minute, she returned with the items he needed to seal up the kidnapper's gruesome message.

"J.P.! What's going on?" The sound of Eve's voice coming from behind a closed door near the back of the room brought his head around.

"Edith's fine. I'll fill you in as soon as I take care of it."

Turning back to the job at hand, he bagged the rat and its wrapper along with the box it came in, put it in the paper sack first, then into the plastic garbage bag and finally the shipping box Edith handed him.

"When does your mail carrier come?"

"This afternoon around three."

"Will you make sure this goes out today?"

"Yes."

Taking the permanent marker Edith handed him, he scribbled the address of the private forensics lab he used in L.A. onto the box. He sealed the package and put it on the corner of the table.

He had to admit it was a stomach-turning piece of evidence, but not one he could overlook. If even a single print was found it would override the howls he was sure he'd hear from his buddy at the lab when he opened the parcel for examination.

Glancing at the desk where Eve's computer sat, he spotted the telephone. "Is that the phone where the kidnapper's call came in to Miss Brooks?"

"Yes."

J.P. reached into his pocket and pulled out the recorder, glad the thug who'd trashed his computer and ransacked his bunk room had failed to take the device.

"What is that?" Edith asked.

"An in-line recording device. Once I plug it into the phone jack and plug the telephone into it, we'll be able to record any call that comes into the lodge. Hopefully we'll catch a break and record one from the kidnapper."

Edith nodded. "What will they come up with next?" She stepped up and took the box off the table. "I'll get this weighed and affix the postage."

"Thanks," he said, watching her gingerly take the parcel from the table and head out of the studio as if at any moment it might break wide open.

Within a couple of minutes he'd installed the recorder.

"J.P.?" Eve called out.

Taking one last look around her cushy prison, he turned and left the studio, headed for the room at the end of the hall to tell her what had just transpired.

The thug had intended to send Eve a message. One he knew would strike at her heart. Feed her fear he'd follow through on his threat if she didn't pay the ransom.

But it wasn't going to happen on his watch. He was here to protect her, no matter what.

This was his fight now.

Chapter Five

J.P. eyed the montage of temporary cowboys as they trailed into the barn, a couple with their saddles slung over a shoulder, all carrying duffel bags for the two-week period they'd be working branding season at the Bridal Falls Ranch.

Rubbing leather soap over the seat of a nice Circle Y saddle with a soft rag, he listened to Devon Hall give each man his bunkhouse assignment and explain the schedule. Only one man blipped on J.P.'s radar. A lanky cowboy named Ted Allen. Something in the way his calculating stare had roamed over everyone and everything made J.P. wonder if he was looking for more than a couple of weeks' pay.

"If you boys wanna head on up to bunk row and get settled in, we'll meet half an hour from now at the corral to pick a mount," Devon said.

A nod went through them as they turned and headed for their accommodations.

J.P. straightened and watched them go, pulling in details before turning to Devon once the group was well out of earshot.

"Locals?" he asked, laying the soiled cloth on the saddle seat.

"All but one of 'em."

"Let me guess. Ted Allen?"

Devon nodded. "How'd you know?"

"I didn't like his calculated once-over. Better keep an eye on him. I'll run a background check on all of them to see if anything turns up."

The ranch foreman pushed his lower lip out in consideration of the request. "Can't hurt. The Bridal Falls Ranch needs temporary cowpokes we can trust." He tapped the folder in his hand presumably containing the temporary workers' employment applications. "But I didn't just ride in on the last stagecoach, J.P. And when this is all over, I'd like to know what the hell is going on and why you're really here."

His nerves bristled as he met Devon's unrelenting stare. He didn't read challenge there, just concern.

"Eve Brooks is in danger. I'm here to protect her while I try to find out who's making her life hell."

The foreman didn't blink. "This doesn't have anything to do with the missing samples from the cryo room, does it?

"It never happened."

"I can live with that. Besides, she's the boss. What she says and does goes. You can come up to my office for these employment files this afternoon while I've got the crew out combing for strays. They'll be in my inbox. Did you find out anything I should know about on my permanent crew?"

"They all came back clean."

"I knew they would." Devon turned and walked away, apparently satisfied for the moment with his answer.

J.P. shrugged off the layer of unease his body was wrapped in, picked up the saddle and carried it into the tack room along with the cleaning supplies.

Eve Brooks was a fragile soul. A fact he hadn't understood until she'd told him about the pipe bomb. Then she'd received the box containing a dissected rat, clearly a message from the kidnapper quantifying his threat to hurt her. She'd taken the information okay, but he'd heard the distinct sound of fear in the tremor of her voice.

Flopping the saddle onto the rack, he left the tack room and headed for the bunkhouse.

She'd survived a nightmare, and what a horrific nightmare it was. He couldn't even imagine what it would be like to have a bomb go off in his face.

Too bad the rat package itself hadn't given up clues as to who'd sent it on the address label, and it would be weeks before he heard back from the forensic lab in L.A. He'd even called the delivery company, hoping someone was able to identify who'd sent the unnerving message to Eve's doorstep, but no one could.

A week on the Bridal Falls Ranch and he was no closer to finding Eve's tormenter than the day he'd arrived.

EVE STARED AT THE GROUPING of photographs arranged on the wall in her work space. Celebrity brides smiled back at her, adorned in flowing waves of taffeta, satin, lace, beading and chiffon precisely wrapped around their figures and personalities. All gown designs she'd envisioned while she'd stared in awe at the beauty of Bridal Falls, with its glistening train of water and veil-thin mist of spray.

She could use some inspiration right now.

Catching her lower lip between her teeth, she glanced at the letter in her hand. Amanda Blackburn's wedding gown request, along with her personal profile. It was due back in L.A. on the cutting floor by the end of the week for a sample gown to be constructed for her first fitting and final approval.

She contemplated her options. She hadn't been comfortable soaking up the falls' particular brand of magic since the kidnapper's calls had started.

But nothing had taken place since the rat incident, and J.P. was never far from her. Maybe it was time to trust him with her safety and the true secret behind her success.

Forcing the weight of doubt from her mind, she pressed the intercom button on her desk.

"Yes?" Edith's reply came over the speaker.

"Please go and find J.P." The words hung up in her throat, but she forced them out. "Ask him to saddle Ginger, and a horse for himself. Tell him I'll meet him in the barn in half an hour. I'm going to ride out to Bridal Falls." She released the button and closed her eyes, praying Edith didn't challenge her wishes with a motherly cajole layered in sympathetic overtures. That would make it all too easy to follow her instincts and retract the request. To stay locked up in here forever.

"I'll take care of it, dear."

Straightening, she shook off the fingers of fear combing over her nerves. Turning, she headed for her room to change into jeans and boots, purposefully avoiding her reflection in the mirror as she passed the open bathroom door.

Thinking instead about the fact she hadn't felt the sun's direct warmth on her skin in months.

J.P. REINED IN THE headstrong bay he'd saddled and slid a glance toward Eve, whose face was skillfully hidden beneath the thick veil hanging over the brim of her hat.

"How far to the falls?" he asked, taking a look at his watch. They'd left the ranch forty-five minutes ago.

"It's three miles from the main lodge as the crow flies. Three and a half this way. My great-grandmother Evelyn discovered it the year she and my great-grandpa Parnell homesteaded the place."

"In 1890 as I recall."

"You've been talking to Henry Brashear, haven't you?"

"He's a knowledgeable man and a good pilot. Sure seems to know and care about your family."

"Yeah, as long as you never ask him about my mother, Katherine."

"He claimed the Brooks women are a hardy lot."

"Not my mom. She hated it here. Left the first chance she got and took me with her."

"Did you grow up in L.A.?"

"Yeah." Eve steered her mare off onto an overgrown path and leaned forward in the saddle. "We've got a steep climb ahead. It'll take us along this ridge before it drops us into a narrow meadow at the base of Bridal Falls."

J.P. tried to relax into the rhythm of the horse's gait, but he couldn't stop watching for movement in the thick stands of timber skirting the trail. There were an infinite number of places to hide, and any one of them could produce a threat he would never see coming until it was too late.

Casually, he felt for the butt of the pistol strapped to his side, the one the thug hadn't discovered tucked under the mattress in his bunk room. Drawing a sense of security from it, he stayed on alert. His Glock was still at large, and deadly in the hands of whoever had stolen it, but at least he knew the ranch hands of the Bridal Falls each had an alibi for the night it was taken. They were all playing poker.

The hiss of water whispered just beyond a cluster of trees, and it turned to a rush as they topped out on the spine of the ridge and began their descent.

He caught a glimpse of the falls through the trees. Intrigued, he sat up straighter in the saddle, anxious to take in the sight. He was no expert on places you had to see to believe, but he knew he'd become a convert the second they cleared the trailhead and reined in the horses on a patch of grass-scattered earth.

"Incredible," he whispered. Unable to take his eyes off the mesmerizing waterfall, he watched it leap from a lip of rock a hundred feet above in a fan pattern. It divided midair into three separate gushers and broke apart on a prominent outcropping of rocks below before flowing into a serene pool thirty feet long and thirty feet wide.

"I was four years old the first time I saw it." Eve dismounted and led her horse to a spot where a makeshift hitching post had been constructed between two trees.

"It was the most magical thing I'd ever seen in my life. It still is." She casually tied her horse's reins around the post and pulled them tight.

"My grandfather made sure I had a photograph of it the following week. Gave it to me in a frame. I still have it."

J.P. climbed down out of the saddle, wishing he could see her expression behind the veiled hat. It was the first time he'd detected a note of genuine pleasure in her voice.

"Were you close?"

"Very. We idolized each other. He was old and I was young. No one in the middle seemed to be paying much attention to either one of us at the time, so we teamed up. When I was old enough he taught me to ride, to shoot, to track wild game, to be self-reliant...." Her voice trailed off, her head lolled forward, and he wondered if she wasn't about to cry behind her veil.

"And he introduced me to this beautiful place. He helped me become who I am, and then he passed away. Less than a year later, my parents divorced, my mother got custody and moved us to L.A. My dad took over the ranch."

"You still miss him, and this place, don't you?"

"Every day." Eve turned to rummage in her saddlebag

and pulled out a large, clear plastic satchel that contained a sketch pad and baggie of pencils. "You're welcome to hike around if you'd like. I've got work to do. Shouldn't take more than an hour."

J.P. stared after her as she headed for a rock near the base of the falls. She was tall and slender, her stride graceful and easy. Natural? Or maybe that had come from her years as a model. Either way, he enjoyed the view.

"You should feel the water," she said over her shoulder. "It's nice."

He watched her step up onto the rock. Heat clouded his brain for an instant. He got lost in her movements, watching her sit down, then cross her legs, much as a child would do. If he could reach out right now and touch her, he would.

Perturbed with his thoughts, he retrained his focus and surveyed the entire perimeter of the area. All the natural beauty made his head spin, but he couldn't let it distract him from his mission of keeping another beauty safe.

He tied up his horse next to hers and walked to the edge of the pool. Squatting down, he trailed his fingers through the crystal clear water and scanned for a bottom in the basin, but he didn't find one.

Deep. Warm. Eighty degrees.

"Geothermal. Spring fed. It's a great skinny-dipping hole," Eve announced from her perch in the center of the rock with her sketch pad on her lap. "My favorite thing to do is leap from this rock into the water."

"Are you speaking from experience?" He pushed back up onto his feet, intrigued by the playful lilt in her voice.

"I'll never tell." She went back to her drawing, and he relaxed, watching her hand work the pencil on the sketch paper.

It was understandable how easily she found inspiration here, with the lulling flow of the waterfall. But could she find peace?

Behind him, a rustle in the brush triggered a full-on response.

He spun around, seeing movement near the opening of the trailhead. Warning knifed through him. In battle mode, he reached for his weapon, his hand frozen on the butt of the pistol.

Less than fifty feet away a bull elk erupted from the bushes and stopped in the middle of the trail.

J.P. tensed, watching the wary animal's large brown eyes take in the perceived threat of intruders on the banks of his watering hole. A big game animal his size could be dangerous, depending on the time of year. Breeding season was particularly tricky, but months away, and with no cow elk harem to protect, he'd probably retreat if challenged.

Glancing Eve's way, he saw that she seemed undisturbed by the presence of an eighteen-hundred-pound beast with antlers. Working his way her direction, he kept his eyes on the animal, putting himself between her and the threat.

The elk snorted, then bolted into the buck brush next to the trail. He reached Eve, still tracking the animal's movements, unable to relax until he moved off a safe distance.

"He wasn't going to charge," she said, still running her pencil over her paper without so much as glancing up. "Rut is months away."

"You do know something about elk behavior. I'm impressed." Impressed that a woman who'd traveled the world in her career, judging by her modeling profile, would know anything about the mating season of bull elk in west-central Idaho.

Glancing down he admired the wedding dress sketch

she'd nearly completed. He wasn't an expert, but he could see the craftsmanship in her lines. "You've got talent."

"Thanks. Fortunately I've been able to parlay it into a business I love. Eve Brooks Bridal Couture. As soon as I send this drawing off to L.A. for her final approval, it'll become Amanda Blackburn's gown for her nuptials to Ryan Taylor next year, oceanside in Malibu."

He let loose a low whistle, doubting she could hear it over the rush of the falls. He'd just seen actress Amanda Blackburn's latest movie on the big screen the week before he'd taken Eve's case.

"Hell of a long way between here and Holly-weird."

"Just the way I like it." With a stylized sweep of her hand, she signed the bottom of the drawing and laid the sketch pad on the rock next to her. "I can't function in that world anymore."

"Because of the pipe bomb explosion?"

"Yes. It flipped my entire world upside down. Do you have any idea what that's like?"

"No," he lied. His world had tilted in the past three years, but Eve Brooks was talking. He didn't plan to stop her with his own tale of redemption.

"*Vogue* magazine, Ms. Brooks, can you look this way? Smile. You're looking a little thin, Eve, are you eating enough? You've got to drop five pounds by Friday's *Harper's Bazaar* cover shoot or the Versace isn't going to hang right."

"Do you miss it?" He considered her calm demeanor, but saw her fingers tremble as she locked her hands together in her lap for a moment before uncrossing her legs and scooting to the edge of the flat rock.

"Sometimes. It was a shallow existence, but I was a part of it for a while. The parties, the glamour hounds, the phenomenal connections. I started out sketching clothes I'd like to wear. Then one summer I spent it here with my dad getting over a case of exhaustion after a long bout with the flu while I was in Paris. A couple of rides out here to the falls alone, and I knew what I wanted to do."

"Change up your life?"

"Yes." Her head turned in the direction of the falls. "Something about the way the water flows from above and thins over the rocks had me seeing tulle and chiffon. Needless to say, I stopped strutting the catwalk and started sketching bridal gowns. With my connections in the fashion world, things took off from there. We grossed over seventy-five million last year."

Caution worked through J.P. as he figured her net worth into the current situation. "It's off subject, but don't you find it odd that Thomas Avery's kidnapper only demanded half a million dollars in ransom money?"

She shrugged her shoulders. "Yeah. It was a pittance for his life."

"A sophisticated kidnapper does his homework. This guy didn't, or his ransom demand would have reflected it."

"You think he's stupid?"

"I didn't say that, but he's more likely to make a mistake that'll get us closer to finding out who he is before he tries to hurt—"

A bullet grazed the skin on J.P.'s left arm.

The sting was instant.

He half twisted, half fell toward Eve, hearing the distinctive crack of rifle report high on the ridge above them.

"Shots fired!" he yelled as he locked his arms around her and dragged her off her perch onto the narrow strip of earth between the rock and the pool.

A scream of protest gurgled in her throat, but she went limp in his arms. "Where?"

"On the ridge above us." J.P. inched up for a look, trying to get a bead on the shooter's location. Movement next to a tamarack tree in a bank of white pine caught his attention. A glint of sunlight against a shiny object, the flit of a blue shirt in a blaze of green foliage. He memorized the location using the tamarack as a landmark and slipped back down.

Round two ricocheted off the top of the rock in a glancing blow.

Eve's sketch pad took the bullet, turned to confetti and spun off the rock in a shower of sharp gravel that pelted them like rain.

"We're sitting ducks if we stay here!" J.P. said. The small meadow was void of trees and places to take cover. Only the shallow flat rock offered any kind of protection, but that wouldn't last if the shooter flanked them. He eyed the falls and the massive outcropping of boulders where the water made landfall.

"The falls, Eve," he said against her ear. "What's behind the waterfall?"

"There's a narrow opening on the left side between the rocks."

If they could reach the rocks and climb in behind the falls, they'd be protected from the gunman. He could return fire if the sniper came within range. Right now, at this distance, his pistol was no match for a rifle.

Another bullet drilled into the ground inches from where their feet poked out from behind the rock.

Eve squealed and pulled her knees up.

"You've got to swim for it, Eve. Crawl in behind the falls. I'll return fire, give you time to make it. Do you understand?"

She nodded, the veil of her hat bobbing in time with her answer.

"I've got six rounds and two reloads. I'll squeeze them

off a couple at a time. Stay under the surface. He'll have a hard time getting a clear shot."

He squeezed her hand. "Go."

Eve's heart slammed against her rib cage. She clawed for the water's edge. Sucking a deep breath into her lungs, she slipped into the pool on her belly.

Pulling with her arms, she reached for depth. The force of the water floated her hat off her head.

Panic bit into her brain, robbing from her oxygen supply.

Turning back for the hat, she heard the first couple of rounds from J.P.'s gun resonate at the surface of the water.

She spotted the disguise suspended like a filmy jellyfish just within her grasp. She reached for it. It slipped through her fingers and floated farther away.

Another loud report fired from J.P.'s weapon.

Her lungs burned, on fire with uncomfortable jolts of tension, warnings that her air was short.

Drowning for a stupid disguise?

Still torn, she turned for the base of the falls and kicked as hard as she could in her cowboy boots. She reached the face of the outcropping below the waterline. Using it as a guide, she pulled herself up the rocks and broke the surface of the water.

Bam-bam. Two rapid-fire rounds blasted from J.P.'s pistol just over her right shoulder.

Terrified, she squeezed through the opening and rolled onto the rough contours of the stone directly behind the falls. It was a place she knew well. A place she'd explored many times, but never with a sniper bearing down on her.

Sucking in one deep breath after another, she felt her heart rate slow before she pushed up onto her knees and crawled into the narrow space on the left side behind a massive bolder, careful to keep her head down in case the shooter fired into the cranny.

Counting the seconds, she prayed J.P. wouldn't get hit by a bullet. She slicked the water out of her eyes with her hands, trying to catch a glimpse of him through the crystal sheet of water in front of her.

Movement at the water's edge signaled his plunge into the pool.

Reaching up, she pressed her palm against the left side of her face. Wisps of horror intertwined with fear, and both conspired to rip her composure to shreds. If only she could erase the scars.

How would J.P. react? Would his assessment be as brutal as Thomas's had been? Oh, he'd soothed her that day in the hospital when the bandages came off, told her she was still beautiful, still his, but she'd watched his dark eyes grow cold. Seen the thinly concealed flare of disgust in them whenever he'd dared to focus on her for more than a second instead of the clock on the wall, or the bed linens.

She closed her eyes against the onslaught she knew was coming. How would J.P. react when he finally got the chance to see what was left of her face? Worse yet, what would he really be thinking behind those incredible blue eyes?

Would she see revulsion darken them like black clouds over the sun, or—

She heard him exhale in a spray of water as he broke the surface and pulled himself through the narrow opening in the rocks.

Tension locked her in place. She braced for his appraisal. Every muscle in her body clamped tight until she knew she'd shatter.

Chapter Six

Thud.

Something slapped against her leg. Her eyes flew open in the misty confines of the rocky crag. Next to her on the stone lay the waterlogged remains of her hat and veil.

"I snagged it when I saw it. I thought you might need it."

Without looking in his direction she snatched up the soggy disguise and pressed it to her face to block his view.

"Has he stopped shooting?" she asked, releasing the tension binding her body so tightly it threatened to crush her.

"He didn't return fire after my last barrage. He's gone, or planning to wait us out and pick us off when we resurface."

Daring a look his direction, she caught sight of blood seeping from an open wound on his upper arm and soaking into the wet fabric of his white shirt.

"You've been shot!" Concern, like a dry towel, soaked up the puddle of trepidation she'd been rolling in.

In one quick motion, she tore the veil from the hat, wrapped it around his arm and tied it to stem the bleeding. "It looks like a graze. We'll call Doc Morton as soon as we get back to the lodge—"

J.P.'s hand on her arm made her jump. She bit down on her words, trading them for her lower lip. Tears dammed in her ducts. He'd seen her face. He was assessing it now, making a judgment call against her, pulling back, turning away.

Eve swallowed hard, feeling the weight of self-loathing threatening to take her down again into a dark place she'd barely escaped from once. She couldn't do it again.

"I'll track down the bastards. And when I find them…" His voice was a low whisper, a threat that pulled her gaze to his in the magnetic connection pulsing between them, alive and heated.

He reached out for her.

She closed her eyes, trying not to flinch as he pressed his open palm against her face.

His touch was tender, therapeutic, bold. She opened the floodgates and released the tears, focusing on the feel of his skin against hers, ignoring the tangle of fear knotting her thoughts.

With painstaking care he smoothed his hand along her cheekbone and down her neck. Everywhere the fiery pipe bomb's reach had found her once-flawless skin.

A shiver quaked through her. She opened her eyes and trained them on J.P.'s, searching the depths of his blue gaze for any sign of repugnance.

Mesmerized, J.P. let his fingertips glide over the contours of her scars. "Skin grafts?" he asked, marveling at the surgeon's handiwork.

"From my back and stomach. The skin there is most like the tissues of the face."

"How many surgeries?"

"Five, and I'll need another one this fall, but there isn't any more the doctors can do for me."

Respect festered inside of him. She'd been to hell and made it out alive, still beautiful and healthy. Part seductress, part girl next door, all woman.

He stared into her eyes, seeing a shadow of doubt emanating from within. She was still gorgeous, and somehow he had to convince her of it.

"I admire your moxie, Eve. Not everyone could have come through a tragedy like that as well as you have."

She flinched against his palm. A brief involuntary reaction to his summation. In that instant he realized the depth of her trauma, of the annihilation of her identity. Someone had to put Eve Brooks back together again on the inside as well as her surgeons had done on the outside.

"You're alive, you're here…and you're beautiful." He let his hand fall away from her face but maintained eye contact, hoping she'd accept the truth from him.

Defiance flickered in her eyes for a moment, then vanished. Her sensuous mouth pulled up into a sad smile. "I've heard that line before."

He wanted to shake her. Make her see what he saw, but it was going to take time. "Thomas?"

"Yeah. The day the doctor removed my bandages. It's a wonder he didn't run screaming from the room." Her smile faded, her gaze turning distant. A single tear made it onto her cheek. She brushed it away. "I know he wanted to."

"Then he's a fool."

"He's a realist, J.P., as am I. Smart enough to know my million-dollar looks disappeared in a matter of seconds next to that California highway. I'm not going to get them back. If I hadn't bent over to pick up the earring I'd accidentally pulled off with the telephone receiver, I'd be dead. As dead as the Eve Brooks brand will be if anyone ever sees my face again. Why do you think I've worked so hard to keep it a secret?"

He hadn't considered the impact this might have on her business. She was the face of Eve Brooks Bridal Couture. But he now knew the bomb had ripped away her veneer and exposed her vulnerabilities.

"You should have contacted the FBI. They would have run surveillance on the drop zone, maybe found the explosive device before you arrived."

Anger shadowed her face. He watched it flare and manifest in the indignant set of her shoulders. Tension tightened her lips. "I wouldn't have called them if they were the last ten people on earth. Their incompetence got my half sister Shelly murdered."

"You didn't tell me about this."

"It happened three years ago in Brentwood."

The blood drained from J.P.'s extremities in hot currents and pooled in his boots. He knew the case like he knew his own soul. He'd agonized over every gruesome detail, replayed every aspect in his nightmares, but he prayed the two cases weren't one and the same. "What happened?"

"She was kidnapped on the way home from college. My mother and stepfather contacted the FBI immediately after the first ransom call. They did exactly what they were told to do." Her voice faltered. "She still wound up dead and dumped outside their front gate like a sack of garbage."

A muffled sob escaped from between her lips as she leaned toward him.

He wrapped his arms around her. "I'm sorry, Eve." And he was. Sorrier this instant than the day he'd been running tactical command calling the shots in the Shelly McGinnis kidnapping, only to have the money drop go bad and the young woman wind up dead.

How in the hell had he walked straight into this buzz saw of fate? How was he ever going to extricate himself from it? Perplexed, he stared through the veil of water into the meadow, where the horses were still tied to the hitching post.

His insides twisted into knots as he tried to ignore the feel of the woman in his arms. He'd been honor bound to protect Eve Brooks the moment he took her case. Nothing had changed with her revelation, and it wouldn't until he knew she was out of danger. Then he'd tell her the truth. He was responsible for her half sister's death.

Raising his arm above Eve's head, he looked at his watch. Forty-five minutes. They'd been hiding behind the falls for almost an hour, and the shooter still hadn't approached their location. He took comfort in the fact, pulled Eve closer for a second, then released her.

"He should have been right on top of us by now, or untying the horses to prevent us from making a getaway."

"You fired back. Maybe he decided it wasn't worth dying for, whatever *it* is."

Looking down into her upturned face, he fought the sudden urge to kiss her. "Until we know for sure he's gone, you have to stay put."

Her eyes widened in panic. "Can't we wait longer? Maybe until dark?"

He considered her suggestion for two seconds, then focused his gaze on her. "It's going to be okay, Eve. I'll swim out, stay low and take cover behind the rock. If he's still up there he'll squeeze off a couple of rounds and try to hit me, but my guess is he took off when I returned fire."

Blinking hard to beat back the tears burning in her eyes, Eve stared up at J.P. He was right. They had to leave the safety of the falls sometime. Better in daylight than darkness when the shooter could stalk them from the brush next to the trail, leaving them no chance to shoot back.

J.P. pulled his pistol from out of its holster and opened the cylinder. "You said your grandfather taught you to shoot. Do you think you can handle my .41?"

"Do bears live in the woods?"

A hint of a smile played over his sexy lips as he gazed

at her with an intensity that made her toes curl inside her soggy cowboy boots.

"I only have six rounds left, so if you have to use them, use them wisely, and not until you see the whites of his eyes, understood?"

"Yes." Burned by the seductive current sizzling between them, she looked down at the pistol in his hands and watched him eject the spent shell casings then finger new bullets into the cylinder.

"You got those wet. They won't work." Concern rode over her nerves.

"The casings are sealed. The gunpowder inside is dry. They'll fire."

Satisfied, she listened to the cylinder snap shut. It had been years since she'd handled a weapon, but she could do this. She could blast a hole in anyone trying to blast one in her, or J.P. for that matter.

"There isn't much recoil with this .41 mag, so don't flinch. Just aim and squeeze off the round."

"Got it." Reaching out she took the stainless pistol from him, feeling its weight in her hand before gently putting the gun down next to her.

"Be careful," she said, reaching for him. She put her hand on his arm. The muscle in his forearm went hard under her touch.

"I always am." He covered her hand with his. "Give me twenty minutes. I'm going to take off on foot to the location where he set up. I need to see if he left anything behind. Anything we can use to help identify him."

Worry cloaked her emotions, but she knew he was right. "What then?"

"I'll be back for you. Watch for me next to the rock. I'll wave my arms, give you the all clear, then you can swim out to me."

She could only nod, knowing if she opened her mouth to protest, the fear churning in her stomach would betray her calm exterior and she would dissolve in a heap.

"Twenty minutes." She repeated the time frame, glanced at her watch long enough to pull herself together and then back up into J.P.'s eyes, seeing his intent in a blaze of blue sparks.

Like two magnets, they leaned toward each other.

A sigh moved up her throat as his lips found hers.

She closed her eyes, lost as a myriad of sensations burned through her reserve like a torch, deepening her need as desire ignited in her body. She was hungry for his touch. Desperate to feel his hands on her skin…desperate to feel like a woman again…desperate to feel.…

J.P. broke the kiss and rocked back, stunned by the intensity. It pounded in his head and radiated through his body like a drug.

"Twenty minutes," he half whispered, half shouted before slipping through the opening in the rocks and into the pool.

Digging with his hands, he reached for depth. What the hell had just happened? He'd kissed Eve Brooks. A mistake, granted, but the best-feeling mistake he'd made in a while.

A mistake he could never repeat.

Eve caved against a shiver and tried to relax the tension in possession of her muscles. Part cool and wet, part J.P.'s kiss, all beyond her control. Staring through the curtain of water, she watched the ripple of his body as he climbed out of the pool next to the rock. Listening, she held her breath, hoping she didn't hear the sound of rifle fire.

Nothing.

Relief spread through her like liquid as she watched him dart to the edge of the clearing and blend with the trees.

She wouldn't be satisfied until he returned unharmed…
or until he kissed her again.

J.P. WORKED HIS WAY UP the slope, ducking for cover every
few yards to listen. A hawk screeched high overhead in a
field of blue, where it soared on a thermal current. A squir-
rel chattered somewhere in the stand of timber, but things
at ground level were still.

Moving another fifty feet, he tucked in next to a massive pine. He scanned the bank of trees where he'd seen
the flash of blue. Nothing moved, but he had to be certain.
Being unarmed could be fatal. Spotting a four-inch-thick
chunk of tree limb on the ground, he picked it up, prepared
to use it like a baseball bat if necessary.

Flanking the cluster of trees on his right, he circled
around to make sure the shooter wasn't dug in somewhere
out of sight, waiting to mow him down in a surprise attack
the moment he stuck his head out.

Clear. Focusing his attention on the ground, he searched
for anything that might offer a clue.

Pine needles, pinecones, tree moss and small twigs littered the soft soil under his boots. Looking up he gauged
the distance to the pool, spotting the flat rock clearly from
where he stood. He had to be on top of the sniper's position.

Combing the forest floor with his gaze, he found what
he'd hoped would be there and stepped closer. Going to his
knees, he studied a single foot impression outlined in the
dirt. Brushing it with his fingertips, he pulled away several pine needles. The shooter was wearing boots, judging
by the pointed tip of the imprint.

Reaching over, he picked up a twig and put it alongside
the track, then broke the stick off at the exact size of the
boot the sniper had been wearing. Matching it to anyone

on the ranch was going to be difficult, but it might help him eliminate any ranch hands who didn't own a rifle.

J.P. pushed up onto his feet and stepped to the right of the footprint. A rifle ejected shell casings, sometimes feet away. It was pretty certain the sniper had picked up the empty casings, but he studied the ground, hoping to catch a break.

"Bingo," he whispered, spotting a glint of brass nestled in a clump of bear grass three feet from the base of the tree trunk.

"Missed one, you SOB." He stepped forward, bent down and picked up the bullet casing. Straightening, he held it up and rolled it between his fingers, gauging the caliber. .308. Today was his lucky day. They'd be one step closer to finding Eve's tormenter if he could get a ballistics match. He shoved the casing into his pocket.

EVE SAW THE SNIPER dart out into the clearing in a streak of blue, muted by the looking-glass sheet of water separating them.

Terror enveloped her as she reached for the pistol next to her.

Had J.P. already encountered the sniper? Was he somewhere on the ridge, bleeding? Dying?

She raised the .41 and searched for the man in blue, the man who'd attempted to kill them.

Next to the flat rock at the side of the pool she spotted him.

A shudder quaked through her body, rippling out from the epicenter smack in the center of her chest. She hesitated. Rage bubbled inside her. It scared the hell out of her, but she tapped into her anger, dialed in a spot just to the right of where the thug stood and squeezed off two rounds, one after the other.

The percussion struck the rocks. Her eardrums rang.

She sucked in a quick breath, laced with the metallic tang of gunpowder. She wasn't going to be a victim today.

She had four more rounds to prove it.

Defiance gelled in her veins and resurrected her courage.

Raising the pistol again, she took aim, but this time she pointed it straight at the dot of blue and squeezed the trigger.

Chapter Seven

J.P. hesitated next to the tamarack tree to listen, desperate to put a measure of certainty to the dull popping sound coming from the clearing below his position.

Pistol shots. Two of them.

Was it possible he'd danced around the shooter, leaving him a path straight to Eve?

A single muffled pop confirmed his concern, and alarm went viral in his bloodstream. He took off down the mountain at a dead run, jumping over brush and limbs, determined to nail the SOB before he pried Eve from behind the falls.

Ready for a fight, he covered the last twenty feet of his descent and launched into the clearing with his makeshift club raised in battle.

Empty.

Caution raked over his senses as he scanned the edges of the perimeter for threats before stepping forward, focused on the remains of Eve's tattered sketch pad lying on the ground next to the rock.

His heart rate amped up, sending waves of panic coursing through him. Pulling in a breath, he fought a barrage of horrific images that flashed inside his head.

A large boar hunting knife was stabbed through Eve's

drawing, pinning it to the ground, but he focused on the smudge of blood smeared across the corner of the page.

"Eve!" In two steps he reached the water's edge and dove in headfirst. Had the kidnapper made good on his threat?

Pushing through the water, he surfaced at the base of the falls. Clawing his way through the narrow slit between the boulders, he prepared for what he might find.

"Ryker!" Eve dodged to the left and pushed up against the rocks with her shoulder. "You scared me!" Taking a deep breath, she willed her heart rate down.

"I heard gunshots." Pulling himself up into a sitting position, he studied her as he slicked water from his face. His eyes shone vibrant blue and alert. His mesmerizing intensity made her want to move closer.

"He came to the water's edge. I took aim and fired."

"You hit him."

Regret stretched across her thoughts and settled in her chest. "I killed someone?"

"Relax. You didn't kill anybody. There wasn't enough blood. You winged him."

"Blood?" A shudder crept through her. She closed her eyes for an instant to get her emotions under control. She'd seen too much blood. The realization she could have killed the sniper moments ago needled holes in the courage she'd managed to muster when she'd squeezed the trigger.

"Don't go soft now, Eve," J.P. said. "If he'd have made it across the pool, I don't think mercy would have been on his mind. He put a hunting knife through your sketch pad."

Fear fingered each vertebra of her spine. "You think he planned to hurt me? Cut me up?"

"I think he would have attempted to if he'd gotten in here."

She tried, but she couldn't swallow past the knot in her

throat. "I want to get out of here. Go back to the ranch. I'm sure by now Edith has alerted Devon that we're overdue. The crew will come looking for us."

"Reinforcements. Nice job. Maybe they'll see the shooter on his way out. Hard to miss a man carrying a .308 rifle, wearing a bloody blue shirt."

"You found a shell casing?"

"Yeah, and a boot track. Not much, but it could get us a lead."

Where was the man who'd kissed her less than an hour ago? She suddenly needed him again. Needed to feel his arms around her. Needed to make a connection with him.

J.P. witnessed the shift, watching desire sculpt Eve's beautiful face and soften her rigid stance as she moved slowly toward him.

Guilt walked over his insides, trampling a blaze of need so hot it stole the breath from his lungs. If he kissed her again, he'd be a goner. He'd never be able to get enough of her brand of intoxication. Better to evade temptation here and now while he was sober.

"About that—"

"Kiss." She eyed him with a seductive glance that set his libido on fire.

"I took advantage. It won't happen again."

Disappointment morphed her features. Her eyes narrowed for an instant before her lips compressed in a tight line.

"I understand. We were both caught up in a Wild West moment, is that it? One hot kiss for the ugly girl before the cowboy swims away." Turning, she picked up her hat, slipped through the opening in the rocks and disappeared beneath the water before he had time to stop her.

"Dammit." Irritation crushed his nerves as he picked up

the discarded .41 and shoved it in the holster at his side. He had the sensitivity of a box of rocks sometimes. He should have kept his mouth shut, but he had no right to want her like this. To need the stroke of her hand on his skin. The silky sensation of her body next to his. She'd realize that fact once he told her about his involvement in her half sister's kidnapping case.

Kicking himself ten times harder than she ever could have, he slipped into the water and went deep, breaking the surface of the pool just as Eve reached out to pull the knife out of her sketch pad.

"Stop!" he yelled as he climbed up on shore. "Don't touch it. It's evidence."

She yanked her hand back and collapsed on the grass.

J.P. scanned the clearing for any potential threat, moved to the edge of the rock and sat down. "I'm sorry."

"Don't be," she whispered without looking up. "I don't expect you to want me. What man in his right mind would? My face is—"

"Dammit, Eve." J.P. winced; a surge of frustration circled through his body in a millisecond. "Is that what you think, that you're damaged goods?"

She looked up. Her blue gaze layered with pain so deep it mirrored the depths of the pool in front of them. His heart squeezed in his chest.

"You don't understand what it's like to have your identity ripped from you. Everything I was is gone. Who could bear to look at me when I can't stand to look at myself? Who could ever live with this?" Reaching up she slapped her palm against the side of her face, partially covering the ruddy patch of scar tissue stretching from her cheekbone all the way down the side of her neck.

Sympathy lodged in his chest. Somehow he had to

change her perception to make it match his. Going to his knees next to her, he reached out and pulled her into his arms.

A shudder rocked her body. She tried to push away, but he held on to her, refusing to let go. "Everyone's looks fade, Eve, by accident, by gravity. It's what's inside a person that matters. It took guts to defend yourself today. It took guts to fight through your ordeal next to that highway. Your will to survive is your strongest asset now. Use it."

Eve relaxed against him. It was hopeless to fight him; he was stronger than she was. Unconvinced, she let his words soak into her brain, but it was his nearness that acted like balm on her soul. How long had it been since anyone had spoken to her with any sort of reason?

Her therapist? Sometimes. Her mother and stepfather? Once in a while. Thomas? Never.

She closed her eyes for a moment, then pushed back and stood up. "Let me have a look at your arm."

He came to his feet and turned his left shoulder toward her. "It's a flesh wound. Probably done bleeding by now."

"Good, because I need my veil back."

Slanting a look in J.P.'s direction, she saw a measure of defeat play across his features.

"What? I'm not going to show my face to everyone. That's my choice."

"You showed it to me." He caught and held her gaze. A cord of attraction passed between them, locking them in its web.

"You're different." Reaching out, she untied the knot holding the veil in place and worked to avoid his eyes. He had her on this one, but she wasn't sure how to explain the new awareness circulating inside her. What did she feel?

Trust? Yes. She trusted J.P. Ryker. With her life and her marred face. Of that she was certain.

Freeing the veil from his arm, she dabbed at the shallow wound. "Any deeper, you'd be in serious trouble."

"Thank you, Nurse Ratchet."

Amused, she turned for the water and rinsed the blood out of the filmy fabric, then wrung it out and shook it free in the afternoon breeze.

Grabbing her hat up off the flat rock, she secured the veil to it and positioned it on her head. She bent over, picked up the baggie of assorted pencils the gunman's bullet had left untouched, straightened and shoved them in her back pocket.

"I'm going to need your satchel for the evidence." He motioned to the knife and her sketch pad.

"Sure." Eve reached down and picked up the bag.

"Hold it open for a minute."

She watched him unfasten the button at his sleeve cuff, then work to pull the wet fabric down around his fingers.

"What are you doing?" she asked.

"Protecting evidence. The shooter had to have touched the handle of the knife. Maybe we can recover a print if he wasn't wearing gloves." Pivoting away from her, he turned his back.

"Oh." Heat rippled through her body as she watched him go to his knees. The fabric of his shirt pulled tight across the broad expanse of his upper back and shoulders, molding to every gorgeous layer of muscle.

Her mouth went cake-flour dry. Annoyed with herself for staring, she turned her gaze on a focal point above him and tried to get her brain to track.

"Eve."

"Huh?"

"The satchel. Can you bring it over here and hold it open?"

"Yeah." Refocused, she stepped close to him and held the bag open, watching him lower the knife slowly in.

"One more thing." He squeezed the remains of her sketch pad in half and forced it, bloody smudge side down, into the satchel along with the knife.

Pushing to his feet, he took the bag from her. "Are you okay? You look flushed."

"I'm fine. Let's ride," she said as she turned and headed for the trail opening where the horses were tied. "I have to get back to the ranch and redraw the gown while it's still fresh in my mind."

J.P. stared after her, unsure if anything he'd said a minute ago had changed her perspective; he hoped it had. Goose bumps erupted on his arms, making him aware the sun had dipped behind the mountains. The air held a decisive bite. It didn't help that his clothes were wet and his weapon almost empty.

Caution worked his nerves. They had to get off the mountain before dusk settled in to obscure their visibility. The shooter could be waiting for them anywhere along the trail.

J.P. hurried to where Eve had untied their horses and put the satchel of evidence into his saddlebag. "Do you think Devon will come looking for us?" Looping the reins over his horse's head, he reached out and hung on to Eve's mare while she shoved her foot into the stirrup and mounted up.

"We're three hours overdue."

J.P. put his boot in the stirrup and swung aboard. "We've got to push these horses if we want to make it home before dark."

Eve nodded, then reined her horse onto the trail and trotted away. J.P. took up the rear, scanning the woods for movement as he listened to the steady clip-clop of the horses' progress.

Devon Hall knew Eve was in danger. He'd told him as much. With any luck he'd come armed with more than a damn pistol. Still, if Eve had wounded the shooter badly enough, he was probably long gone by now and seeking medical attention somewhere. The possibility could provide them with a clue to his identity. The closest hospital in Cascade would be required by law to report a gunshot wound to the police.

In the distance the spiking notes of a wolf's howl raised another round of cold creeps on his arms and across his chest. Tapping his heels against his horse's flanks, he moved up alongside Eve, determined to come between her and anything they might encounter on the trail.

"What's the matter, city boy? Never heard a wolf call?"

"Something like that." He was pretty sure she was grinning under her hat. "I can belt out a mean wolf whistle, but I'm more concerned by the prospect of coming face-to-face with a man and his .308."

Reaching up, she flipped the veil up onto the brim of her hat and shot him a worried glance. "You think he's that determined to kill me?"

"I'm not sure." They topped out on the peak of the ridge and started their descent along its spine, riding side by side in the gathering dusk.

"But it seems unlikely he'd shoot you if he wanted you to pay the ransom."

"Maybe he was aiming for you."

J.P. considered her suggestion. Granted, he would have to be lying on a slab before he ever let anything happen to her. But who knew that? Who knew with him out of the way, Eve would be vulnerable?

"Who knows I'm here to protect you and find the kidnapper threatening you?" he asked, breaking right with her onto the main trailhead.

"Edith and my parents who are in Europe for the next month."

"What about the friend who referred you to me, Tina Davis?"

"I didn't give her any details."

"That leaves Devon Hall who knows you're in some sort of danger."

"Well, someone else has to know. I'd trust Edith and my folks with my secrets, and I have."

The trail turned hard to the left, but Eve reined in her horse. "Whoa. Do you hear that?"

"What?" J.P. pulled back on the reins and sat taller in the saddle. "Hoofbeats. Coming up the trail toward us."

"It could be Devon," she whispered.

Concern sluiced in his veins. "Take cover."

Without hesitation, she maneuvered her horse around behind a clump of buck brush and pulled up short.

He urged his mount around the twist in the trail as a riderless horse trotted toward him. Devon Hall's horse?

"Hold up," he urged the animal, catching the blood bay by one of the loose reins swinging from its bridle. "Easy," he coaxed, watching the horse's eyes widen in fear. "Eve."

Trotting out onto the trail, Eve stopped her mare next to J.P.

"That's Devon's gelding, Hannigan." She stared down the trail in front of them. "He had to have come this direction." In the descending darkness, her eyes picked out a form sprawled in the middle of the path.

"Look! There he is." Worried energy infused her body. She spurred Ginger forward, only to be stopped when J.P. reached out and caught one of her horse's reins before she could move past him.

"Whoa, Eve."

"I'm not a horse." She glared at him, doubting he could

even see her expression in the gathering gloom. "He's injured!"

"Yes. But I can't let you go charging down there and maybe right into the sniper's trap. We don't know who knocked him off his ride."

She sobered. He was right. It could be some sick trick, conjured to draw them in so he could take them out.

Reaching back, J.P. popped the snap on his holster and withdrew the pistol. "Take this."

Reaching out she locked her hand around the butt of the pistol.

"I'll use Devon's rifle." He leaned out over Devon's horse and pulled a long gun out of the saddle scabbard. "Better odds."

Eve nodded, and together they urged their horses forward at a trot. She watched the left side of the trail. J.P. covered the right.

They reached Devon's motionless body in a matter of minutes.

"You check him out. I'll stand guard."

She handed J.P. his .41, and he slipped it into its holster. Climbing down out of the saddle, she hurried over and went to her knees next to Devon Hall. Even in the gray-dark, she could see he'd been clubbed on the right side of his head. Blood oozed from a nasty gash resembling the end butt of a rifle. It was surrounded by deep bruising. He'd taken a vicious blow to his brain. Fear skated over her nerves, carving desperation into her thoughts.

"Devon! Devon, wake up. It's Eve. Devon, can you hear me?" Reaching out, she pressed her hand to his shoulder, feeling his warmth penetrate her palm. A good sign.

"Devon," she coaxed, giving him a gentle shake.

A low moan rumbled from her ranch foreman, followed by a string of garbled words.

She shook him again. "Devon, it's Eve. What happened?"

"He's been here awhile," J.P. said as he scanned the surrounding woods for the sniper, then dismounted, rifle in hand. "The blood had time to coagulate. Devon must have ridden into our shooter right after the man left the falls."

Kneeling down, he pressed his middle and index fingers to Devon's wrist, feeling a strong pulse thump under his fingertips. "Good pulse, but he's going to need a ride in the back of an ambulance and recovery time."

Putting the rifle aside, J.P. worked his arms around the ranch foreman and gently dragged him up into a sitting position. "Devon, buddy. Can you hear me?"

"Damn right…what the…" Devon listed to the left, but J.P. steadied him before he could tumble over.

"You were bushwhacked, Devon. My guess is with the butt of a .308."

"We've got to get him back to the ranch. I'm responsible for this. If anything happens to him…" Her statement trailed off, leaving the guilt in her voice to ruminate inside his head. He studied her outline against the night sky.

For all of her financial might and ability to keep her face hidden from the world, she still cared about others over and above her own insecurities. A chink in her mask? A way to change her perception of herself?

A shout in the distance brought his attention up. He reached for the rifle next to him.

"Hall! Devon Hall!"

The thud of horse hooves on the trail out in front of them accompanied a blade of light.

Eve scrambled to her feet, recognizing the deep note in Tyler Spangler's voice. "Tyler! Over here."

"Miss Brooks?" The flashlight beam swept out past them, then pulled back, finally settling on their location.

"Holy cow." Tyler reined in his horse and bailed out of the saddle. "What happened to Hall?"

"Are you alone?" J.P. eyed the cowpoke in the glare of the flashlight beam Tyler had trained on Devon.

"No. Buck's a furlong back and Ruckus is with him. We've been combing the woods for y'all since nightfall."

"Thank goodness," Eve whispered as she reached up and pulled the veil down over her face. She'd gotten so wrapped up in trying to help Devon, she'd forgotten to hide her tragedy.

"He needs medical attention," she said, infusing her voice with a note of authority she didn't quite feel. "Ride out and find Ruckus. Send him and Buck back here so we can get Devon on his horse and keep him there. Then head for the ranch and call an ambulance. I want it there by the time we arrive."

J.P. stared up at Tyler. "Call the sheriff while you're at it. Devon was assaulted."

"This wasn't an accident?" Tyler asked.

"No, it wasn't. Someone deliberately tried to hurt him."

Eve straightened her spine, thankful J.P. was willing to involve the county sheriff. It could help them discover who'd done the shooting.

Tyler handed her his flashlight, shoved his booted foot into a stirrup and climbed aboard his big bay horse. "I'll ride as hard as I can, Miss Brooks."

"I know you will."

Tyler spurred his horse forward and gave him his head. The powerful animal lunged into a gallop.

Eve squelched a shiver, watching horse and rider melt into the darkness like an apparition, leaving only the clatter of hoofbeats behind them. Had Tyler Spangler seen her face? Stared at the ugly scars marring her skin, with the intention of informing every cowboy from here to Timbuktu, that the beautiful Eve Brooks wasn't so beautiful anymore?

A scintilla of acceptance skated across her nerves. Did it really matter what anyone else thought in the scheme of her life? Puzzled by the reflection, she turned back to where J.P. sat next to Devon, holding him upright. She sank to her knees next to them, to wait for Buck and Ruckus to come, and prayed Devon Hall was going to be all right.

Chapter Eight

Red and white strobe lights flashed across the ranch's structures, giving them a citified feel. The sensation took root in the pit of J.P.'s stomach. This place was pristine, innocent. But not tonight, not under the threat of sniper fire and bodily harm. It felt too much like L.A.

The EMTs helped Devon Hall onto a gurney and loaded him into the back of the ambulance, where they checked his vital signs and put a precautionary neck brace on him to stabilize his spine.

Eve had been whisked away by a frantic Edith Weber the instant they'd dismounted and tied up their horses next to the barn. It was better for her to remain above the fray, at least for now. But they'd set up a rendezvous time for later, after things wound down.

"J.P."

"Yeah." He turned to find a breathless Tyler Spangler standing next to him.

"The sheriff's office is dispatching a couple of deputies, one here to the ranch and one to the hospital."

"Good. Maybe he can track the bastard who did this with the evidence I collected out at Bridal Falls."

"But Devon wasn't anywhere near the falls when you found him."

"Someone took some potshots at Miss Brooks and I

this afternoon at the falls. He left a hunting knife stabbed through her sketch pad. Took off after the incident, and less than an hour later we found Devon in the middle of the trail. The two attacks have to be linked. Hall must have stumbled upon him."

"Damn," Tyler whispered, his gaze turning toward the back of the ambulance.

"I only hope he saw the thug before lights-out and he'll be able to identify him."

"You J.P. Ryker?"

He glanced up at the EMT framed in the rear doors of the ambulance.

"Yeah."

"You can speak with Mr. Hall now, but we roll in a couple of minutes."

"I won't be long." He stepped up and climbed into the back of the vehicle then took a spot on the bench seat parallel to the gurney.

The medics had raised the gurney into a sitting position, making it easier for him to see that Devon Hall looked like hell under the overhead lighting. The swelling caused by the blow had steadily expanded to include his right eye. Only a sliver of iris peeked out from between the puffy lids.

"They're going to patch you up, Hall. You'll be back in the saddle in a couple of days." He studied the ranch foreman, who'd been bobbing and weaving in and out of consciousness like a jaywalker through L.A. traffic. Not a good sign. He had a concussion.

"Sheriff Adams is sending a deputy to take your statement at the hospital in Cascade."

"Ain't much to state. I never saw the SOB who hit me."

J.P. leaned closer. "Can you remember anything, Devon?

Anything at all? A sound, a feeling. Was he on horseback or on foot?"

Hall closed his good eye for a moment, leaving J.P. to wonder if he'd lost him to coma, or recall.

Devon's good eye flicked open. "Rifle butt. Saw it out of the corner of my eye a second before the impact rattled my jaw."

"Anything else? Anything that could help us nail this bastard?"

"Blue." Devon cleared his throat. "His shirt sleeve was blue."

Tension coiled around J.P.'s nerves, leaving him ready to strike. All the evidence suggested the sniper had been on foot. He'd never heard the distinct thud of hooves. It would have been much easier for the thug to hide, to lay in wait until the target got within striking range. Now he knew for certain the shooter who'd tried to take them out was the same man who'd assaulted Devon Hall along the trail.

"The crew, Devon. Can you account for each and every one of them?"

"Dang right. We pushed cows all day. Cleared the west pasture."

"Does that include the temps you hired for branding?"

"Every one of 'em."

A couple of thumps on the side of the ambulance signaled the driver needed to roll.

J.P. stood up, stepped to the rear of the vehicle and climbed out. "Hang in there, buddy. Someone will be in to check on you at the hospital in the morning."

"Okay." Devon raised his hand in a single wave and closed his good eye.

The EMT secured the rear doors, went around to the driver's side and climbed in.

J.P. watched the ambulance roll away with the Bridal

Falls foreman in the back. It could just as easily have been Eve or himself, if they'd even survived the gunshot. Bone tired, he realized it had been one mean day and they'd all survived.

So far.

He turned and headed for the hitching post where he'd tied up his horse. The deputy would arrive soon, and he planned to turn over the knife and bloody sketch pad to the officer along with his statement.

A measure of doubt glided across his nerves. Next he'd have to convince Eve it would be okay to bring in the local authorities on her case. More pairs of eyes on the situation would be a good thing, not to mention the resources that could come along with them.

The hitching post was empty.

"Hey, Ryker, wait up," Tyler hollered.

J.P. slowed his pace until the cowboy caught up. "Where are the horses?"

"The crew put them up an hour ago."

He nodded but couldn't squelch the rising worry in his bloodstream. "I've got this, Spangler. Just need to get something out of my saddlebags."

"Sure. I'll hang out and wait for the deputy to get here."

"Yeah." Focused on the entrance into the barn, he listened to Tyler move away from him and cross the driveway behind the lodge.

Light glared inside the massive barn from a series of overhead fixtures hanging from the ceiling. Horses shuffled in their stalls, still agitated by the evening's events.

J.P. headed straight for the tack room and the saddlebags his horse had carried.

Stepping inside, he flipped on the light switch next to the door and spotted the saddle he used on the rack next to Eve's.

A tantalizing mental image swam in his head, of her beautiful face in a sheen of water, the feel of her lips. His blood stirred hot and heavy.

Anxious to dial back the increased hammering of his heartbeat, he pushed the image out of his mind as he stepped in next to the saddle. Reaching out, he undid the buckle on the leather bag on the right side. The evidence it contained could blow his investigation wide open and possibly lead him to the kidnapper.

The hairs on the back of his neck bristled as he eased his hand into the bottom of the bag.

Empty.

Frustrated, he leaned across and unfastened the buckle on the left-hand side, reached in and found it empty, too.

"Dammit." Rocking back, he eyed the bags on Eve's saddle. There wasn't a chance it was there, but he checked anyway. Empty, too.

"Ryker! Deputy's here," Tyler hollered from somewhere behind him.

He gritted his teeth, turned and left the tack room. Was it possible the shooter still lurked somewhere nearby in the cover of darkness? Had he waited for an opportune moment to steal back evidence that could convict him?

Stepping out of the tack room, he spotted Tyler Spangler's retreating back as he exited the barn. It could just as easily have been someone on the crew.

Caution edged his thoughts as he walked toward the deputy standing next to his rig. Eve was in more danger now, and he could use all the help available. Including the local authorities.

Digging into his jeans pocket, he pulled out the shell casing. At least he still had it, and within a few minutes it would be in the hands of the local authorities.

EVE PUSHED BACK IN THE porch swing and filled her lungs with night air. There was no veiled hat tonight. No scarf wrapped strategically across the top of her head and over the remains of the left side of her face. Instead, she'd applied a series of pressure dressings over her skin grafts. It was an option to total exposure and she'd made her peace with it upstairs in front of the bathroom mirror, but it was also the catalyst for the decision she'd made tonight.

She heard J.P.'s approach before she saw him, boots rustling across the grass, then tall and imposing against the light of the stars overhead.

"So this is where you hole up at night when you're not out galloping around."

"Pretty much." She patted the seat next to her and gave up a measure of emotional cover as he sat down on the swing. Every nerve ending in her body started to drum, and she was instantly aware of the length of his thigh pressed against hers.

"I wonder how Devon is doing." She knew he was in good hands at the hospital, but she needed an entrance into a conversation she intended to steer.

"I'll find out in the morning right after I meet with Sheriff Adams."

An involuntary shudder rippled through her. "I didn't want the locals involved in the kidnapping threats. I wanted to maintain a level of anonymity. How far into this are you going to drag him?"

"As far as necessary. Devon's assault and the potshots the assailant took at us up at the falls are both well within his jurisdiction. We can't prevent him from investigating now that someone has been hurt. He might even bring in a forensics team to try and recover bullet fragments if they can locate them."

"I know one dang near took the toe off my boot."

"Dang near?" His voice held a note of curiosity. More a question than an observation.

"What? You don't think that's close enough? I like my toes. I'm glad they're still attached."

"He could have drilled me with his first shot. He got the drop on us. He had a scope on his rifle. That's how I spotted his location on the slope."

"You think he intentionally missed? Why would he do that?"

"It raised the threat level in your mind. Could be a psychological game. I can take you out anytime I want, therefore you better give me what I want, or else."

"He let us live, but he bashed Devon's head in?" Fear attached itself to her nerves, growing a knot in her stomach.

"Devon was in the right place at the wrong time, or maybe something a little more simple. Devon may have been able to identify him if he'd have come across him on the trail."

Eve sucked in a labored breath and let it out slowly, feeling tension lock the muscles tight between her shoulder blades.

"There's something else you need to know."

"What?"

"The knife and sketch pad we recovered went missing tonight from my saddlebag."

A groan escaped from between her lips and set her pulse to pounding in her chest. "He could be here right now? On the ranch?"

"Yes."

"I'm coming with you into town tomorrow." Had those words really come out of her mouth, she wondered as she picked out a particular star in the night sky and trained her eyes on it.

"Are you sure?"

"Yes. He's my foreman. He works for me. It happened on my land. It's the least I can do." Apprehension glided through her. She hadn't been to town since her arrival at the ranch in the cover of darkness. Too many questions, too many challenges, not enough courage.

"Then you'll need to fill out this written-statement form tonight so I can give it to the sheriff in the morning."

"Okay." She reached out and took the folded sheet of paper from his grasp. Pulling herself together, she shifted her focus on J.P., desperate to avoid the myriad of conflicting emotions certain to tag along on the trip.

"I've made another decision. As long as this creep is at large and willing to perforate me, us, I want you to move into the lodge. I'm going to have Edith prepare the room down the hall from mine." She hesitated, waiting for a refusal that never came. Instead he sat in the darkness next to her and remained silent.

Flustered, she pushed up from the swing and went to the railing at the edge of the porch. With her back to him she offered up the confession that had stirred in her mind since the day he'd arrived at Bridal Falls Ranch.

"You make me feel safe, J.P. I know I can trust you to be honest with me."

"That, and I've seen your face."

"Exactly." Shoot, she'd stepped in a puddle of his extreme reasoning again.

"You don't have to work to convince me, Eve. You hired me. I'm here to protect you. If you wanted me to stand guard on the peak of the barn roof in my boxers, I'd be obligated to comply."

She turned around, watching him come to his feet in front of her like some sort of ancient warrior. A jolt of desire liquefied in her veins, sending need throughout her entire body. Thanks to him and that kiss behind the falls this afternoon, she knew there were parts of her left that were still all woman.

"Tomorrow morning then." He moved close to her, so close she could smell the desire coming from his body. Warm, male and charged with sexual heat.

He tipped his hat and stepped off the porch.

Sucking in a breath before she passed out, overheated on passion, she hurried to the front door of the lodge, pulled it open and stepped inside.

"WAY TO GO, RYKER," he scolded himself as he finished a third trip around the perimeter of the barn, working to get his raging libido under control in the crisp night air.

Wanting the boss wasn't in his play book.

Worried, he tried to determine if desire had replaced his sense of duty where Eve Brooks was concerned. If so, then why in the blazes had he ever consented to move into the lodge?

He turned north and headed for his bunk room. She was well within her comfort zone, asking him to move closer for protection's sake. It didn't matter that she'd just breeched his.

He clamped his teeth down on a string of profanity decidedly aimed at his own lack of control. He would have kissed her again tonight, but for one nagging truth.

She claimed he made her feel safe. Would she still feel that way if she knew the truth about his role in her half sister Shelly's kidnapping case? Or just how tragically that sense of security had worked out for her and her family?

Devoted to his internal rant, he nearly collided with Tyler Spangler halfway between the barn and bunk row.

"Ryker. What are you still doing up?"

"I could ask you the same thing." Eyeing the ranch hand, he noted the .22 rifle clenched in his hands. "Hunting?"

"Nah. My cow dog, Hank, took off from the porch an hour ago and hasn't been back. I'm hoping the wolves didn't get him."

"Maybe all the action around here earlier scared him off."

"It's possible," Tyler speculated. "He'd be hiding out in the garage. He's got a favorite spot in there. I'm gonna have a look before I turn in. Night, J.P."

"Good night." J.P. watched the newly appointed foreman of the Bridal Falls Ranch, at least until Devon Hall's return, stride off into the darkness toward a bank of vehicle garages.

Caution jumped in his system as he calculated the odds the shooter might be wandering in close proximity.

It was unlikely, and he was beat. He needed to turn in. He took several steps forward and came to a stop. "Dang," he muttered, then turned around to help Tyler Spangler find his missing dog.

"You look exhausted," Eve said as she climbed into the SUV the next morning.

"Spent a good hour after we talked last night searching for Spangler's dog, Hank."

"Did you find him?" she asked.

"Nope."

"He's old. Maybe he wandered off to die? Animals do that."

"Could be." He slid her a sideways glance, noting the way she'd expertly used a sheer scarf to conceal the flesh-tone bandages on the left side of her face. She wore large-rimmed sunglasses, putting him in the mind of Jackie O. If he didn't know better, he'd say she could pass for a movie star.

Looking away, he shifted the rig into drive, maneuvered out of the garage and into the driveway.

"How far to town?"

"Just over that mountain." She pointed to a sizable peak and smiled. "Thirty miles as the crow flies, sixty miles on this road if you take a right."

"Now I see why you employ a helicopter pilot." Grinning back, he pulled out onto the main road and stepped down on the accelerator for the uphill climb away from the ranch.

"Is your room satisfactory?"

He mentally considered the new accommodations he'd moved into this morning inside the lodge. "One hundred and ten percent."

"Good. I also had Edith order you a new laptop."

"That wasn't necessary, but thanks."

"You're welcome. Besides, you can't be expected to sleuth without an internet connection."

She had a point. She'd offered him the use of the computer in her studio, but he had no intention of disrupting her every time he needed to work. Especially when he started digging around in the background of people she loved.

Looking into the rearview mirror, he watched a beat-up red Ford pickup pull out of a gated driveway and roll up behind them.

"Tell me about Thomas Avery's position at EBBC?"

"He's chief of operations and my chief financial officer. I gave him contractual control over a large share of the company when we got engaged, but I still hold the power to dissolve the partnership."

"Ever considered going back?" Glancing at her, he tried to get a read on her expression but came up short. Grieving for what once was usually accompanied tragedy.

"I'll eventually have to. I'm the CEO and lone designer."

"Any regrets?" It was none of his business, but he didn't seem to be able to stop the barrage of questions circulating in his mind this morning.

"Plenty." She turned away to stare out the window of the moving vehicle, presumably to gather her thoughts.

J.P. gritted his teeth. Thomas Avery didn't have a clue what an incredible woman he'd shunned. Anger kindled inside him against the man who'd so callously trampled her fragile persona. If he ever came face-to-face with the bastard, he planned to let him know how far over the line he'd stepped.

He eased off the gas pedal and steered the vehicle around a sharp turn. Slotting the SUV through a narrow pass, he drove over the summit of the mountain Eve had pointed out and off into heaven.

"Would you look at that," he whispered, staring at the rugged peaks of a range that stretched for eternity.

"You don't see that in L.A." Slipping a quick glance in Eve's direction, he watched her smile.

"I love it here. It's so beautiful, it's easy to forget there's a whole other world out there."

"I can see why." Awestruck by the spectacular vista, he angled for a wide pullout on the left side of the highway and stepped on the brake.

It went to the floor under his booted foot like a squashed grape.

Concern zipped over his nerves. He hit the pedal again. Nothing.

Eyeing the speedometer, he watched it tick up and pumped the pedal a couple of times, hoping it might bring the fluid level up in the brake line. Still nothing.

"Dammit!" Reaching down, he grasped the gearshift lever and pulled the transmission into low. The motor over-revved. The RPM needle shot up into the redline, where it stayed.

"J.P., what's going on?" Eve asked, caught off guard by his series of quick moves and the unnatural scream of the SUV's engine. Reaching up, she took off her dark glasses, folded the earpieces and squeezed them in her hand.

"We've got no brakes."

Terror cut through her nerves, but she held them together. "Try the emergency brake!"

J.P. pulled up on the lever situated in the console between them, but the SUV didn't slow.

"It's been disabled! Hang on. We're in for a wild ride to the bottom."

She choked back a gasp, focused on the series of S turns in front of them. She knew this stretch of highway and visualized the rest of it in her mind, until she hit an insurmountable obstacle that rocked her forward in her seat.

"You have to ditch!"

"What?"

"A mile ahead there's a series of switchbacks. Jackknife corners. We won't make them." She stared at the speedometer. "Not at this speed." She didn't have the heart to tell him there were half a dozen more just like them midmountain.

Sweat formed across J.P.'s forehead, tiny biting beads of concentration as he fought to maintain control of the runaway vehicle carrying them toward certain death.

Eve was right. Their only chance of survival was to ditch before they reached the switchback.

He took the next sweeping right turn, cutting it wide as he feathered the gas pedal, giving the SUV just enough acceleration to shift its center of gravity and nail them to the corner.

"How many more sweepers before a jackknife?"

"One."

He flashed her a quick glance. Their gazes locked. Fear clouded the normal pristine blue of her eyes and made him want to touch her. "Hang on, sweetheart."

Turning his focus on the road ahead, he made his calculations and roared into the last turn before doom. Reaching for the gearshift, he rammed the transmission into Park.

The wheels locked up, grinding tread on asphalt, slowing them a fraction as the transmission disintegrated underneath them. Cranking the steering wheel hard to the left, he put the rig into a controlled skid and drove it nose first toward the embankment. J.P. shut his eyes at the last second before impact and heard Eve scream.

The high-end SUV slammed into the mountainside. The air bags deployed around them.

Chapter Nine

Eve recoiled back into her seat and dared to open her eyes in the chaos. A wall of white surrounded her. Struggling to get her bearings, she mentally searched for injuries to her body and found none.

No blood, no guts, no gore.

"J.P.?" Worry worked through her thoughts, conjuring one horrible image after another until she thought her heart would explode in her chest. "J.P.!"

"I'm right here. Are you okay?"

Reaching out with her hands, she pushed them against the partially deflated air bag in front of her and shoved it back.

"Nothing hurts, nothing broken."

"Good."

She watched J.P. grab the door latch on his side and pull.

"Jammed shut. Try yours."

Yanking on the handle, she felt the latch give. "Mine works." She pushed the door panel open, popped her seat belt and climbed out, thankful for the feel of terra firma under her feet.

Three steps forward and her knees buckled. Going with it, she sank to the ground next to the crashed vehicle and started to shake.

J.P. unfastened his seat belt and clawed his way over

the console into the passenger seat. Spotting Eve on the ground, he slid out of the SUV, took a couple of steps and went to his knees beside her.

"Remind me to get one of these someday. It's built like a tank."

Turning a watery blue gaze on him, minus any amusement at his joke, she burst into tears.

"Ah, sweetheart." J.P. pulled her into his arms and felt her tremble. She'd been through hell and back once before. This incident had no doubt stirred up those memories.

"We're both okay."

"Emm," she squeaked.

Holding her back, he fingered her chin and gently raised her face so he could look at her. With the flick of a finger, he brushed her tears away, wishing she'd smile.

"We made it. There's nothing to cry about."

Eve swallowed the lump in her throat and trained her focus on him. He was right. They were safe and the SUV could be replaced. Working to pull herself together, she used those two facts like glue and cemented it with the feel of his fingers on her skin. Heat arced through her body in a blaze so hot it incinerated any concerns she had left.

"I know," she whispered, staring into his half-lidded gaze.

In slow motion his mouth found hers. She melted against him, savoring the salty flavor of his kiss. With her tongue, she teased open his lips.

She was starving to feel his hands on her body, crazy for his touch in dark, secret, emotional places no man had reached before.

Toot…toot! The blast of a horn severed the forbidden kiss and brought J.P.'s head up.

He barely made it onto his feet before Eve had the scarf once again secured over the left side of her face. Reaching down, he pulled her to her feet and turned to where a man in a red pickup pulled to the shoulder of the highway. It was the same beat-up red Ford he'd seen behind them shortly after they'd left the ranch.

A man in his early fifties climbed out of the pickup and hurried toward them. "I'll be damned. Are you both okay?"

"We're fine. Air bags and seat belts." J.P. studied the good Samaritan, noting he wore a pair of leather gloves, a jacket and cowboy boots. He looked like a rancher.

"J.P. Ryker." He extended his hand and they shook. "This is Eve Brooks."

The man tipped his hat. "Howdy, Miss Brooks. Glad to finally meet you in person. We're neighbors. My spread, the Clayton Ranch, sits against the southwest corner of the Bridal Falls."

"Oh. You must be Roger Grimes, Edith's nephew. I've heard so much about you."

"All good, I hope." Grimes looked her over, a slow sweep of a stare that riled the hairs on the back of J.P.'s neck and put him in defense mode.

"I'm headed into town for supplies. I can drop you there if you'd like, give you a chance to call a tow truck."

J.P. considered the offer. The SUV wasn't going anywhere. He was pretty sure the fan had perforated the radiator, not to mention the transmission he'd sacrificed in his effort to slow the beast down and minimize the crash. They were at least twenty miles from the ranch. Too far to walk.

"We'd appreciate that." Once the SUV was in a garage, he planned to have a mechanic take a look at the braking system. This was no accident.

An odd look of anticipation passed across the man's weathered features, as if he'd just won a prize he'd yet to collect.

Yeah, Eve Brooks could do that to a man. He was living proof.

"Let me clear off the passenger seat for you, then we'll get going." Grimes turned and hurried to his pickup.

J.P. watched him go and instinctively reached for Eve. Drawing her close to him, he put his arm around her shoulders. "How well do you know him?"

"I don't know him personally. Just the things Edith has told me about him. I know his wife died three years ago from cancer. The medical bills involved in her treatment were extensive. He was forced to sell off a good portion of his ranch. My father bought it just before he died."

"Does he ever come around the lodge?"

"Yeah, every once in a while, but Edith always goes outside to speak with him. Why all the questions? Do you want to walk home?"

He stared down into her upturned face, trying to decide exactly what was precipitating the hesitation roughing up his nerves. Could be the fact that Grimes was wearing thick leather gloves and a jacket. It had to be seventy degrees standing here in the sun. Or maybe it was the once-over he'd given her.

"Stay here. Something's not right," he whispered before he released her and walked to the pickup, catching sight of Roger Grimes's wide-eyed glare through the driver's side window, as he quickly maneuvered something in behind the bench seat and pushed it back in place.

"Mr. Grimes." J.P. worked his way along the driver's side of the rusted-out pickup, staying close to the bed of the truck. "We've decided to stay put here on scene. Will you call us a tow truck when you get to town?"

Grimes looked up at him as he hoisted a toolbox over the side panel into the bed of the truck. A box full of fencing tools and loose coils of barbed wire. Gone was the friendly vibe from moments earlier. His features were stone-cold as he stared at J.P. across the span.

"It'll be 'bout three hours. Can Miss Brooks make it?"

"She's tougher than she looks."

Grimes nodded, his expression never changing as he backed away and shut the passenger side door of the beat-up Ford.

The air was charged with palpable hostility. J.P. breathed it in, felt its sharp spines darting off Roger Grimes like porcupine quills. Resentment toward Eve Brooks? He wasn't certain, but being forced to sell most of his land to the Bridal Falls Ranch out of desperation could make a man angry. But how angry?

The sound of an approaching vehicle brought J.P.'s head around. He focused on the road as a black flatbed truck appeared, then slowed and pulled in behind the Ford.

He didn't recognize the rig, but he did recognize the man behind the wheel and the Bridal Falls Ranch logo on the door panel.

Tyler Spangler hopped out of the truck, his face contorted with concern. "Ryker, what the hell happened? Are you and Miss Brooks okay?"

"We lost our brakes and had to ditch, but we're both fine."

Glancing at Roger Grimes, he watched him slink around the nose of his pickup.

J.P. stepped back from where he stood next to the driver's side door.

"Thanks for stopping, Roger. We'll catch a ride with Spangler and call a tow truck."

Grimes nodded but didn't look up. He grabbed the handle and opened the driver's side door a fraction. Just wide enough to slip inside.

For a brief second, J.P. focused on the junction where

the back met the flat of the bench seat and the tip of a rifle barrel winked just before Grimes pushed it out of sight with his gloved hand and crawled inside.

Grimes fired up the Ford, flipped a U-turn on the highway and drove back up the hill. The opposite direction he'd claimed to be heading.

J.P. focused on Grimes's pickup until it was out of sight, then let out the breath trapped in his lungs. Had Grimes been stowing the rifle, or retrieving it?

Agitated, he headed for where Eve stood next to the SUV, with Tyler right behind him. "What gets you this direction, Spangler?"

"My dog, Hank. I found him this morning in the weeds behind the garage. Someone wrapped a piece of barbed wire around his snout and tied his paws together with another one. He's cut up pretty bad. I'm headed for the vet in town to get him patched up."

"That's horrible! Who would do such a cruel thing to an innocent animal?" Eve asked as she walked toward them, her brows drawn together in disbelief.

"Someone who didn't want the dog to alert anyone to his presence. Someone who needed time to tamper with the brakes on your SUV in the garage last night." J.P.'s deduction was focused on the fencing tools in the back of Roger Grimes's pickup, and something else that had been bothering him. Grimes never asked what had caused them to wreck.

Maybe because he already knew.

"You think someone intentionally wanted to run you off the side of this mountain?"

"Yeah, but they had to get through Hank first." His muscles went taut as he considered the implications and the rifle on the front seat of Grimes's pickup.

"Hank is a friendly cuss. He'd let anyone give him a pat."

"Including Roger Grimes?"

"Especially Grimes. He gave Hank to me three years ago, after his wife died and he thinned his herd. One less mouth to feed, he said."

J.P. sobered and sucked in a deep breath. The pieces were beginning to fall into place, but there was a problem. How did he take Grimes from disgruntled neighbor to sniper to kidnapper? There was a lot of territory to cover among the three extremes.

J.P. PICKED UP THE BAGGED .308 shell casing off the corner of Sheriff Adams's desk and held it up.

"I found this a hundred yards up the ridge from Bridal Falls an hour before Devon Hall was assaulted."

"I've read the statement my deputy took from you last night and the one Miss Brooks submitted this morning." The sheriff rocked back in his chair and clasped his fingers together on top of his head. "You say someone fired on you and Eve Brooks, she then returned fire with your pistol, possibly hitting the shooter, who was wearing a blue shirt?"

"I'm positive she winged him. There was a smudge of blood on her sketch pad where he'd stabbed the hunting knife through it."

"The one that went missing from your saddlebag?"

"Yes." Frustration sizzled across his nerves, but he held his professional expression intact.

"Your claim is substantiated in Miss Brooks's written statement. Any idea who'd want to hurt either one of you?"

"I've got my share of enemies, but they're not from these parts. Miss Brooks, however, has received numerous phone calls from the kidnapper who nabbed her business partner in L.A. just over eight months ago. He wasn't able to collect on the ransom, and he's threatening to cut her up if she doesn't pay now. He went as far as to send her a dissected rat."

"Where's the carcass now?"

"I sent it out to a private lab for analysis. Should have results back anytime."

"You think he's here?"

"That shell casing and our lack of brakes this morning on the backside of that mountain pass certainly indicate he could be. The mechanic at Boulder Creek Garage half an hour ago found the emergency brake cable cut clean through and a nail-sized hole punched in the brake line on Miss Brooks's SUV."

Frustration glided over J.P.'s nerves. Involving the locals came with risk. They either believed you and got behind you, or puffed out their bulletproof vests and undermined your investigation. He wasn't sure on which side of the line Adams would drop.

"I'll get this brass to my ballistics people, but we've got nothing to compare the shell casing to. Devon Hall did indicate in his interview someone hit him with the butt of a rifle. If his wound pattern matches up with a comparable .308, we'll be searching for that gun."

"Thanks, Sheriff."

"As far as the telephone kidnapping threats and the dead rat are concerned, it's a federal case. Outside my jurisdiction. Best contact the FBI."

He nodded, satisfied with Sheriff Adams's deferment. Small departments rarely had the manpower or the expertise to pursue a kidnapping case. Better to leave every aspect to the feds.

J.P. pushed up out of his chair and centered his hat on his head. "One more thing. Eve Brooks's neighbor, Roger

Grimes. There could be some bad blood between him and the Bridal Falls Ranch over a land purchase some years ago. He wears cowboy boots, about a size ten, comparable to the track I found near the shell casing."

"This is cowboy country. Everyone wears boots."

"He carries a rifle in his pickup. I saw it this morning."

"Half the ranchers between here and the state line carry a rifle, Mr. Ryker. But I'll have one of my deputies check it out."

"Thanks, Sheriff."

"No need to thank me. Just make sure you keep Miss Brooks safe."

"I will." Reaching out, he shook the sheriff's hand and left the office, headed for the pickup, where Eve was waiting. Climbing into the driver's seat, he fired the engine then turned to look at her, unable to see her exquisite eyes behind the dark sunglasses she'd donned.

"Adams is going to take a look at Grimes. His body language up on the mountain this morning was suspicious."

"I hope you're wrong about him, J.P. It's going to get really awkward between Edith and I the moment she realizes we gave the police her nephew's name."

He put the truck in Reverse, backed out of the parking space and rolled to the edge of the lot. "I'll be there to look out for you."

"Can you take dictation?" A note of amusement intertwined with her question.

"If I have to." Shooting her a sly grin, he pulled out onto the street in the ranch truck and headed for the hospital where they planned to pick up Tyler from his visit with Devon Hall on ranch business. Branding was set to start tomorrow, about the time Devon could be sprung from the hospital and Hank could be picked up from his night at the veterinarian's office.

"Have you considered the possibility that Edith could somehow be involved, or at the very least, feeding her nephew information?"

"Yes. But why would she betray me? She knows I care about her. I trust her. She's the only person on the ranch I told about Thomas's kidnapping, and what happened to me. She's the only one I've been able to confide in about it."

"You're a hundred percent sure about how you feel?"

"I am, and that's why I plan to withhold judgment until we know for certain. Give her the benefit of the doubt. Perhaps she's simply a gossip and inadvertently gives Roger the details of what goes on around the ranch."

"That's the best approach." He didn't doubt it. Let the evidence tell the story minus conjecture. But the lifeblood of his security business was speculation, and he'd done plenty of it since their encounter with Roger Grimes this morning.

"I called the pilot from the hospital after our visit with Devon," Eve said. "He's warming up the chopper to take us back to the ranch. We'll have Tyler drop us at the hangar."

"As the crow flies works for me." He maneuvered the truck into the hospital parking lot, where he spotted Tyler Spangler waiting outside the main entrance. He was glad they'd be taking the chopper back to the ranch instead of driving. He planned to get the lay of the land around the ranch from the air and have Eve point out the Clayton Ranch and its proximity to the Bridal Falls.

Until there was provable evidence Roger Grimes was somehow involved, he couldn't rush to judgment, relax his guard or overlook a potential suspect, no matter how unlikely they appeared.

THE SOUND OF THE HELICOPTER's blades calmed Eve's frayed nerves. She pulled the scarf tighter against her face, adjusted her headset and relaxed into the seat next to J.P., anxious to get home. Home? The Bridal Falls Ranch had become her home. That fact had somehow married with the feeling it was her only home, and she didn't want to consider being anywhere else, including L.A.

"Good to have you aboard, Miss Brooks." The pilot's voice echoed in her ear.

"It's good to be aboard, Henry." Henry Brashear had been her father's chopper pilot since her early teens, and she instantly enjoyed the air of familiarity.

"Once we get to the ranch, I'd like to give J.P. an aerial tour, if you don't mind."

Henry tapped the fuel gauge. "Topped off the tank as soon as you called, Miss Brooks."

Content, she touched J.P.'s leg to get his attention and pointed out the window. "That's Penny Springs. We used to camp there overnight and play in the hot pools."

Gazing to the north, she picked out another landmark she recognized. "That's Thunderbolt Mountain Lookout. My dad and I hiked up there one summer and spent a week on fire watch. We saw some amazing thunderstorms and lightning shows."

"What's the elevation?"

"Eighty-six hundred feet plus."

J.P. leaned past her to view the points of interest out of the helicopter's small side window, but his gaze locked on her face and glanced off the smile on her full lips.

She'd removed her sunglasses and folded them in her delicate hands. Wisps of her silky blond hair flared from under the scarf and brushed her shoulders. Enthralled by the lilt of reminiscences in her voice, he knew he could listen to her speak from now till eternity and not get tired.

Intrigued by his out-of-place internal rhetoric, he wondered if this was what had brought Thomas Avery into her life? Even scarred, Eve Brooks was the most beautiful woman he'd ever seen. No doubt Avery had come to the same conclusion without ever taking a true look inside her heart.

"Have you ever given Thomas Avery this sightseeing tour?"

Caught off guard, she turned to stare at him, her glacial blue eyes narrowing in contemplation. "I tried, but he wasn't interested. He's been to the ranch many times, but not since my accident. He always tiptoed around like he was afraid he might step in something while wearing his Salvatore Ferragamo shoes."

"A real metrosexual L.A. male?"

"Yeah. That's his breed. Designer rags, fast cars and not a hair out of place, even with the top down."

"Did his time in the storm drain after the kidnapping reshape his attitude at all?"

"No. He's worse." She broke eye contact and turned to stare out the window. "His date with near death only made him want more."

J.P. considered Thomas Avery from Eve's perspective. They both ran in some pretty glamorous circles, so how had Thomas found his way into hers?

"How long has he worked for you?"

"Since just before my half sister Shelly was taken."

"Three years?"

"Yeah. He came to the table with an MBA from Harvard Business School. I snapped him up."

"When did things turn romantic between the two of you?" An uncomfortable knot turned in his stomach. He felt like some sort of psychological voyeur, prying into her love life, but he needed to question her about Thomas Avery. In fact, he found it odd that Avery had been the target of the kidnapping instead of her.

"A year and a half ago. We'd been dating casually and decided to make it exclusive. He proposed a couple of months before he was kidnapped."

J.P. considered the information, boiling it down to a grand total of nothing. It sounded like Thomas Avery had been an easy target with a rich girlfriend. Nothing special.

"Bridal Falls Ranch straight ahead."

"Oh, shoot, Henry, I'm sorry, I didn't mean to drag all my baggage out." Embarrassment clutched in her chest and flared on her cheeks in hot pools she couldn't brush away. She'd lost hold of her tongue and answered J.P.'s questions as if they were the only ones in the aircraft.

"Not a problem, Miss Brooks. I turned down the volume on my headset right after Mr. Ryker used the word *metrosexual*. I figure it's better if I don't know anything about that."

Eve glanced at J.P., seeing a smug grin turn his mouth up in measured amusement. There was nothing metrosexual about J.P. Ryker, and she couldn't be happier. Long, lean thighs wrapped up in tight jeans and a button-down shirt with the sleeves rolled up above his muscled forearms beat the hell out of Armani any day of the week. And his lips? Thomas had never kissed her the way J.P. did.

"Show me the Clayton Ranch," he said, jockeying closer to her so he could look at the ground below.

"Do you see that cabin perched on the ridge?" Pointing, she made sure his gaze tracked to the exact spot. "That's the main house where Grimes lives. The other outbuildings and barn are on that lower flat."

"I see it. How big is his spread?"

"I'm not sure, but my daddy bought three-quarters of it. I'd guess it's about five hundred acres now."

He sat back in his seat, making her immediately miss the pressure of having him close.

"Henry, can you take us out over Bridal Falls?" she asked.

"You've got it." He banked the chopper slightly north-east and hummed over the lodge.

Picking out the beginning of the trailhead, she pointed to the ground. "That's the path we took when we left the ranch."

J.P. eyed the layout. "Grimes could easily have skirted the ranch from his place and gotten the drop on us from the slope above. On foot, in a straight line, he could have beaten us there with half an hour warning."

"Yeah. That's about the time between when I told Edith I intended to go and the time we rode out."

A chill skated through her. Reaching over, she looped her arm around J.P.'s and let his nearness infuse her body with the sense of security she craved. At what point had she become such a poor judge of character? She'd told Edith the details of their trip to the falls. Had she relayed that information to Grimes? "Take us home, Henry. It's getting late."

"You've got it, Miss Brooks."

Chapter Ten

J.P. slugged his pillow a couple of times then shoved it back under his head, trying to get comfortable again. He hadn't been able to go back to sleep since hearing the telephone ring in Eve's room fifteen minutes ago.

Was she talking to Thomas Avery? That was his guess.

Not more than five minutes after Henry had landed the helicopter to drop them off, Edith Weber had come out of the lodge to announce Thomas had called several times for Eve and it sounded urgent.

He closed his eyes, listening to the rise and fall of her voice in the room across the hall where the conversation reached a crescendo, then faded to silence.

Swinging his feet over the edge of the bed, he sat up to listen.

Nothing.

Nothing but crickets and the disquieting bawl of calves in the field outside drifted in on the breeze coming through the crack he'd opened in the bedroom window.

Was she okay? What did Thomas Avery have to say that was so urgent it couldn't wait until morning?

Frustrated, he flopped back onto the bed. He could protect her physically, but not emotionally.

The crush of gravel in the driveway outside brought him up again, but this time he flicked open the window blind and stared outside, seeing the brake lights of the ranch's flatbed truck. He glanced at the clock on the bedside table.

It was almost midnight and Tyler Spangler was just now pulling into the drive? He'd been headed out of town at the same time they'd lifted off in the chopper around four o'clock. Something must have happened to delay him.

J.P. stood up, grabbed his jeans and slipped them on. He pulled on his shirt, grabbed his socks and boots, then tiptoed out of the room and down the stairs, where he let himself out into the main lodge and out onto the porch. Taking a spot on the steps, he pulled on his socks and boots, then headed for the pickup.

"Spangler. What's going on? Where have you been?"

"Damn, J.P., you scared the hell out of me." Spangler flicked the flashlight in his hand onto J.P.'s face.

"Sorry." Lowering the beam, he refocused on the truck. "Someone tried to kill me tonight, and they dang near succeeded."

Caution bubbled inside J.P. He stepped closer. "Let me guess, rifle fire?"

"Yeah, half a dozen rounds. Took out the headlights and one of the rear dually tires. There wasn't a chance I was stopping to change it."

"How'd you make it home without headlights?"

He followed Tyler around the pickup, where he spotted three bullet holes in the passenger side door panel.

"I used this flashlight. Aimed it at the road in front of me. Damn glad I put new batteries in it this morning."

"Where'd this happen?"

"Top of the summit in the narrow pass a couple of miles from where you burned in the SUV this morning."

Uneasiness flooded his system, floating one troubling thought in his head. "Whoever fired at you thought Eve and I were in the truck. They were after us."

"Are you in some kind of trouble?" Tyler's brows pulled together.

He shook his head, unwilling to let the cowpoke in on the truth of why he was really here. "We need to contact Sheriff Adams in the morning and file a report."

"Sure thing."

"I'll pull that dually tire in the morning."

"No problem."

"Night, Spangler. Glad you made it home in one piece." He nodded and headed for the lodge with his nerves on fire. He could almost bet whoever had failed to send them over the side of the mountain had tried to get another shot at them, unaware they'd found another way home ten thousand feet above the fray. He could only hope the gunman's bullet was still lodged in the tire.

He pulled open the screen door and went inside, then locked it behind him. Three feet from the door leading upstairs, he heard the distinctive plink of glass shattering.

"Eve!"

Jamming the skeleton key into the lock, he turned it.

Crash! The hollow ping of more glass breaking echoed into the stairwell.

Taking the treads two at a time, he flipped on the light in the hall as he ran past the switch plate.

"Eve!"

He hit the door leading into her studio and turned the knob. Locked.

"Eve!"

Silence.

Digging in his pocket, he pulled out the skeleton key and fit it into the keyhole. It turned. He pushed the door open.

Light shone from a single lamp in the sitting area on his right.

Smash!

Turning at the sound, he bolted for the door standing ajar at the back of a wide corridor. Eve's bedroom?

Ready for battle, he pulled up short and pushed open the door.

"Don't do it, Eve," he coaxed, watching her lift a large framed photograph of herself standing next to a pretty boy he guessed was Thomas Avery off the wall and drop it on the floor.

The picture joined the rest in a heap of shattered glass and twisted frames.

She turned to stare at him for a moment without seeing him. Tear lines tracked down both her cheeks, still wet in the soft light coming from the lamp on her bedside table.

Turning back to the wall, she reached out and grasped the last framed photo of herself.

He didn't try to stop her. She needed to purge. Gritting his teeth, he watched her lift it off its hanger, raise it and drop it on the floor.

"What happened?" He walked through the doorway into the mayhem. Glass crunched under his boot soles as he moved toward her. Looking down, he saw her bare feet poking out from under the hem of her filmy blue night-gown. Tiny pinpricks of blood glistened on her skin where shards of glass had cut into her.

"Don't move, sweetheart," he whispered, focused on her body as she stood trembling like a blade of grass in the wind. His mouth went dry, his stare fixed on her naked silhouette outlined beneath the flow of her gown.

Glancing down at her flawless image staring up at him from the floor, he worked to get his inflamed senses under control.

"I can't look at her anymore," she whispered. "I don't know who she is."

"I do." He took another step toward her.

"Thomas says my brand is finished. *Elle* magazine is going to publish a feature about my mysterious exit from L.A. and my accident. He says it will bring down the company. He wants to interview other designers."

"I'm sorry, Eve." One more step and he reached her, then picked her up in his arms, high above the sharp angles of glass. He wouldn't have her hurt anymore.

She clung to him. A guttural sob shook her willowy frame and rocked his heart.

He pulled her closer. She was shattered like the mass of her images broken on the floor at his feet. He silently cursed Thomas Avery as he turned and carried her from the bedroom and out into the sitting area.

Easing down onto the sofa with her in his arms, he cradled her until the storm passed. He lost track of time as he stroked her hair and cupped her head against his chest.

Caught up in the feel of his strong body molded around hers, Eve relaxed for the first time in what felt like months. There were no emotions left inside her. Thomas had hollowed them out and she suddenly doubted he'd ever really loved her. He'd been in love with the persona of who she was before the pipe bomb. He was nothing like J.P. Solid and good, formed by reason and honesty.

With her ear pressed to his chest, she listened to the steady beat of his heart for a moment before she pushed away from him and leaned back so she could see his face.

"He wants a meeting in L.A. next week. Lawyers on both sides, etcetera, etcetera, etcetera."

Concern masked his features and turned his eyes bright with speculation. "What do *you* want, Eve?"

She knew what she wanted, and it had nothing to do with a meeting in L.A. "I agreed to sit down at the table with him and his suits."

J.P.'s gaze went neutral, but a telltale tic played along his jaw, making her want to reach up and smooth it away. To reassure him she was no newbie when it came to matters of business. But of the heart? She was just getting started.

"Are you going to let him bully you into hiring someone else into a business you built from the ground up?"

"I didn't say that." It was a mistake, but she let her gaze slide to his lips for an instant before pulling it back to meet his hot-blue stare.

Unchained for the first time from her former self, she leaned into him and pressed her lips to his. A shudder pitched through her body. She raised her arms and wrapped them around his neck.

Melting into him, she triggered a low moan deep in his throat, and the hollow place in her soul began to fill.

J.P. DABBED AT THE CUTS on Eve's feet with a cotton ball soaked in hydrogen peroxide.

She flinched each time he brushed one of the dozen tiny pricks, but she didn't pull away.

"Sting?"

"A little."

Short of a mental pry bar and the willpower of an Olympian, they'd barely made it out of that kiss with their lips still attached. Guilt had plowed deep into his gray matter and forced him to pull back. He didn't want sex with Eve for sex, even though their mutual response, if acted upon, could easily have landed them in her bed.

"We need to get the glass cleaned up before you go back in there." He motioned to her room.

"About that." She nibbled on her lower lip. "You never should have burst in on my pity party. I'm pretty sure I locked the door."

"What's a good cathartic purge between a woman and her protector? I'm here to keep you safe, even from yourself." He watched a sweet smile play across her lips and had to look away. He was ten excruciating minutes away from the coldest damn shower on the planet. He couldn't lose it now.

"I'm going to sleep here on the couch. I'll clean it up in the morning. I'll wear my cowgirl boots." Her brows arched in amusement. "I promise." She studied him from under her lashes, before her eyes opened wide.

"Hey, how'd you get your boots and jeans on so quick?"

"Talent." Damn, he'd almost forgotten the ordeal Spangler had gone through tonight. "I was already dressed when I heard the glass breaking."

"You were downstairs?"

"Yeah. Tyler rolled in around midnight and I went out to see where he'd been."

Her expression changed from silly-overtired-happy to alert employer. "He was right behind us when we took off from the airport this afternoon."

"Someone ambushed him in the narrows at the top of the grade and blew out the headlights on the truck, shot out a rear dually and left three bullet holes in the passenger side door."

She sucked in an audible breath and stared at him. "You think they were trying to hit us, don't you?"

"Looks that way. Someone assumed we'd be in the truck tonight on our return trip."

"Tyler could have been hit, or worse, killed."

"There's a chance the slug might still be in the dually tire. If I can recover it, we'll have rifling evidence to match the bullet to a specific gun. I've got a hunch it'll be a .308."

Eve reached out and pulled the blanket off the back of the sofa, then tucked it up around her shoulders. "Maybe I should just give the kidnapper the ransom money he demanded and be done with it."

"Maybe. But what do you do when he comes back for more?"

"I don't know."

Eyeing J.P. where he sat on the edge of the ottoman with her feet in his lap, she smiled at him, noting the gentle way he'd doctored her injuries. "You better turn in. The first day of branding is always a doozy."

"Yeah." He clasped her ankles in his strong hands and positioned them on the cushion next to him, then pushed to his feet. "Are you sure you don't want my help clearing the glass so you can sleep in your own bed tonight?"

"I'll be fine right here." She watched him pick up the bottle of peroxide and a handful of cotton balls and put them on the table next to the lamp. "Don't bother to lock my door. I'm done hiding."

He paused to look at her for a moment, a mix of curiosity and worry playing across his handsome face, but then he smiled. "Good night, Eve."

"Good night." She closed her eyes and listened to his retreating footfalls on the hardwood floor, until the door closed behind him.

Opening them again, she stared at the ceiling, remembering the feel of his body tangled up with hers. The tender way he'd stroked her hair had unintentionally fanned a flame of need in her body. Hot embers that still smoldered, one kiss away from ignition and total burn.

Somehow she couldn't imagine not having him at her side in L.A. when she fed Thomas his Gucci tie. She would ask J.P. to come with her in the morning.

A thread of apprehension wove its way along her spine. She rolled over onto her side. It eased somewhat, but an annoying stitch of it remained. Going back to Los Angeles scared the hell out of her. It was the kidnapper's stomping ground, but apparently, so was the Bridal Falls Ranch. She wasn't safe anywhere, except in this room with J.P. down the hall. Besides, how was she going to put herself out there again in the land of beautiful faces? It was a place where she no longer fit in.

She listened to the whoosh of rushing water come on in J.P.'s private bath. Settling her head on the pillow, she closed her eyes and homed in on it. It was a normal sound, an everyday sound, a comforting sound.

J.P. REACHED UP AND SHUT off the cold water valve on the shower, noting a hint of blue deep in his fingernail beds. At least some parts of him had taken a hint from the icy water; too bad it wasn't the single part he needed to cooperate.

If he were at home in L.A., he'd try lacing up his shoes and heading for the beach to run himself senseless. It was pretty hard to focus on much when he was fighting for one more mile. That was the only M.O. that had seemed to erase his pain since the Shelly McGinnis case. But he wasn't in L.A. He was here. Fifty steps and an unlocked door from Shelly's half sister and a confession he wished he could run from.

Irritated with himself for churning it up, he pulled the shower curtain back and reached for the towel hanging on the rack next to the tub.

The explosion of glass close by grabbed his attention, but it was the sound of Eve's instantaneous shriek that brought him back to his current problem.

J.P. bailed out of the tub and wrapped the towel around his waist. His heart hammered in his chest as he beat a wet trail to her door, turned the knob and burst in.

Eve stood near her design table with her hand covering her mouth.

"What happened?" He studied her as he stepped closer, seeing the fist-size hole in the plate-glass window and the shards spread in a fan pattern on the floor. Realization shot through him as he assessed the scene.

"Someone just threw this through the window."

Caution worked through his body. "Watch the glass."

She nodded and stepped back. "I tried to see who did it, but it's too dark outside. No porch light on this end of the lodge."

"It's a rock." He studied the fist-size object and the brown paper bag wrapped around it and secured with a thick rubber band. He had to give the pitcher credit; a stone was the best way to get a message to Eve.

"Crude, but effective." Careful to avoid the chunks of glass, he stepped closer, bent down and picked up the rock with his free hand. With the other one, he held the towel securely at his waist.

"It weighs a couple of pounds."

"A caveman's .308?" she said, glancing up at him. "What?"

"Nothing." He wanted to chuckle at her amusing reference, but he fought the urge with a straight face. This lob over the castle wall had come with a message attached. One he doubted either one of them was going to find funny.

"Open it," she urged, eyeing him where he stood.

It didn't take a rocket scientist to see a degree of heat darken her blue-eyed gaze as it flicked across his lack of clothing and the towel around his waist.

"I'll do it." Eve reached out and plucked the rock from J.P.'s open palm, welcoming the distraction from his broad shoulders, six-pack abs and narrow hips.

Unwinding the rubber band, she pulled it off and peeled the thick brown paper from around the hefty stone. "I'm destroying evidence, aren't I?"

"Possible fingerprints, maybe some epithelial cells, but

my guess is he wore gloves, and a badger-hair loincloth when he handled it."

"And I thought I was a smart aleck."

His sexy lips pulled up in a grin. Her knees went to jelly as she mentally melted into the floor. She sobered and opened the note.

"It's a ransom demand. It says, 'Have the half a million in unmarked bills. Put it in a stainless steel briefcase. Not a duffel bag. Wait for my instructions, or you die.'" She rebelled against the fear clamping down on her nerve endings.

Taking a step back, she found the back edge of the sofa with her rear and leaned against it to keep from swaying on her feet.

"It's him. It's the same man who took Thomas."

Caution burned through J.P.'s blood. He knotted the towel at his waist, reached out and slipped the note from her fingers.

"You're sure?"

"Yeah. The phrasing is the same. His verbal instructions to me the first time he called were for me to have the half a million in unmarked bills, and to put it in a stainless steel briefcase. Not a duffel bag. He made the same demand the first time he contacted me in L.A."

"The briefcase request is unique, coupled with the duffel bag reference, but it's not uncommon for a kidnapper to ask for unmarked or untraceable bills."

"He used the same last line, too. Wait for my instructions, or he dies."

J.P. studied the nondescript note cobbled together from random sources. Virtually untraceable, but he'd tell Sheriff Adams about it anyway along with the bullet-riddled truck in the garage.

This kidnapper was a hell of a long way from Los Angeles. Surely a stranger in these parts would have drawn someone's attention by now. So what were the odds the kidnapper was right here?

Judging by the events of the past two weeks and the ransom note in his hand, he had to believe the odds were better than good. But it was going to take a clever offensive strategy to draw the kidnapper out into the open.

"Sheriff Adams won't agree to handle this ransom demand. He's going to insist we contact the feds."

"No! Not the FBI."

"Relax, Eve, I've got no intention of bringing them into this. I'll send it out to the lab for analysis. Maybe they can find something."

She nodded, her fearful gaze locked with his.

"You're planning to participate in branding tomorrow, aren't you?"

"Yeah." Fear flashed in her blue eyes for an instant as he watched her battle back the debilitating emotion. "I've been riding herd in it since I was a teenager."

"Do you think you'd be willing to address the crew tomorrow morning?"

Pushing off the sofa back, she turned away from him.

Concern put him in motion. He set the ransom note down and reached out, pressing his hand against her back.

"I know it won't be easy," he said, feeling her tremble. "But we might be able to use it to draw the kidnapper out."

She turned around slowly, and he let his hand fall away.

"An explanation is long overdue. I'm pretty certain they all know I sneak around the ranch in the cover of darkness, but they're all too respectful to question it."

Tears flooded her eyes, but they stopped short of spilling over when she blinked them away.

His heart twisted in his chest. Every nerve ending in

his body tuned in on the fear he knew coursed in her bloodstream.

"I can do it if—"

"No. It's my responsibility. The crew deserves to know what's going on and why Devon is lying in the hospital right now. It has to come from me."

Reaching out, he pulled her into his arms. She came willingly and pressed her cheek against his bare chest as he circled her in his arms. Desire burned through his body in red-hot swells.

"I'll be right there with you, Eve."

"I know you will." She pushed back and stared up into his face. "Help me get the words right, so we can nail this bastard."

Chapter Eleven

J.P. tightened the cinch and looked up to where Eve worked to saddle her mare.

"Whoa," she coaxed.

The horse tossed her head for a third time and pawed the floor of the barn with her hoof in a show of agitation. The gentle talk seemed to be having no effect.

"What's gotten into you, Ginger?" Reaching out, she stroked the mare's neck. "You're already working yourself into a lather. Better save it for the catch pen."

"Does she usually act up?" he asked, coming around his horse to see if he could help.

"Never. She's just excited with everything going on this morning."

"Easy, girl." J.P. reached out and put his hand on the mare's neck, feeling the slick of sweat on her coat. "Maybe she's picking up on your nervous vibe and working toward a tizzy. Maybe you should saddle another horse."

"Once I get her out in the pasture, she'll calm down. I'll lope her in a circle for a while after I speak with the crew."

"Okay." He stared at her across the saddle seat as she worked the cinch, noting the flesh-tone pressure dressings she'd applied over her scars. "You look good this morning. I'm proud of you."

Her gaze flicked up to meet his, an exaggerated swallow moving the cords in her delicate neck. "I may as well dive in. First day of the rest of my life and all that. We'll see how it goes."

"You shouldn't discount courage, Eve. It took guts to come out here without your veil, and more to inform them about what happened to you."

"Thanks for the pep talk, Kemosabe, but it's nothing that heroic. I've come to the realization that the Thomas Averys of this world can kiss my patootie. I've got to learn to face down people's stares and answer their questions without malice. They're just curious."

"That's what I love about you, Tonto. You're not afraid to speak your mind." He grinned at her, gritting his teeth against the overwhelming arrows of attraction darting between them in a volley he'd already lost.

She lifted the stirrup off the saddle horn and lowered it against the horse's side.

"Have you had your mare long?"

"About five years. My dad purchased her for me when he bought part of the Clayton Ranch. Roger Grimes sold off some of his horses along with his livestock. She was a champion reining horse in her day." Reaching out, she patted the mare's neck. "Competed nationally. You'll get to see her work the herd today. It's amazing to watch."

He couldn't agree more, but his focus was on Eve. Her genesis had begun, and it was incredible. No veil to hide her face, and a cowboy hat shoved low on her forehead. Eve Brooks was a fighter, a champion in his book.

"I finished my background check on the Bridal Falls temp cowboys this morning."

"Find anything?"

"Everyone came back clean, with the exception of one. Ted Allen. He has an outstanding warrant in Montana for failure to appear stemming from a barroom brawl he was involved in."

"We'll keep him out of the bar." She raised an eyebrow and pulled her horse's reins free from the hitching post. "He'll be gone in a week. I'll give him his paycheck and release him from the crew as soon as the first half of the calves are ear tagged and branded."

"Fair enough." J.P. untied his horse, turned him around and climbed into the saddle. "Still, I'd like to keep an eye on him." The memory of the way Ted Allen had given everything in the barn a once-over bothered him. The man had also been the one who put his and Eve's horses away the night the knife and sketch pad went missing out of the saddlebag. He'd shake his uneasiness once the cowpoke rode off into the sunset.

"That's why I'm glad you're here." Eve shot him a quick glance, liking the way he carried himself on horseback. Tall, but relaxed, muscled thighs pressed against the sides of the saddle, knees slightly bent, boots hooked in the stirrups, as if maybe he'd been born there. "I know I can count on you to keep me safe, no matter what."

Fighting a wave of heat as intense as a blowtorch, she shoved the toe of her boot into the stirrup, reached for the saddle horn, pulled herself up and swung her right leg over.

"Where'd you learn to ride?"

"I was raised in a small town in Northern California called Tehama. Do you know it?"

"No." Grasping the reins, she steered Ginger for the wide exit out the front of the barn. "What's it near?"

"Chico."

"I know where that is. The Sacramento Valley. Farm and ranch country."

"Most fertile soil on earth."

Together they trotted out into the morning sun and

reined the horses due south toward the catch pen where the ranch crew was beginning to gather.

"So how'd you get to Los Angeles from there?"

"I drove."

"Cute, Ryker," she scolded, enjoying their easy rapport and his spontaneous sense of humor. "My friend Tina Davis who recommended you said you used to work for the FBI."

"Yeah. Before I started my security company." J.P. sucked a hard breath into his lungs. He didn't want to go down this path. There was risk involved if she innocently stumbled into his admission like a pedestrian into oncoming traffic. They'd both get wrecked.

"What department were you in?"

"I worked a tactical unit."

"Ah, a strategist. That's why you're so good at what you do now."

Relief pumped through his veins. "Let's just say, Uncle Sam's training dollars served their purpose." His nerves went slack, but tension remained locked inside his muscles, refusing to relent, reminding him the day would come when he would have to tell Eve the truth about Shelly's death.

Eve maneuvered Ginger through the main gate Tyler Spangler held open and reined in her horse on the other side to wait for J.P. Her nerves were frayed, but a beat of confidence pulsed in her veins.

"Thanks, Tyler." She nodded to him. "If you don't mind, I'd like you to gather the crew for me before they ride out."

"Sure, Miss Brooks." He secured the gate, climbed aboard his horse and trotted off in the direction of the catch pens.

"You've got this, Eve."

Settling her focus on J.P., she gained a measure of calm

from his surety. He'd be right there with her, but hanging on the outside of the group. Watching for the slightest tell amongst the crew. Any sign that could lead them to the one responsible.

"You're right." She flashed him a grin and reined her horse for the gathering of cowpokes a hundred feet away.

J.P. nosed his horse in behind hers and pulled the big gelding up short a couple of lengths and slightly to the right of where she stopped Ginger in front of the gathering of cowboys.

From his vantage point, he could easily see each man's expression as they shoved their hats back to look at Eve.

"I know there's plenty of work to do this morning, so I won't keep you long."

He sized up each man's level of comfort, assessing the way some of the crew relaxed into their saddles. Some crossed their wrists atop their saddle horns and leaned forward, expressing interest in what she had to say, while others simply stared at her, transfixed, a measure of awe on their faces.

"I've officially put Tyler Spangler in charge until Devon returns. You'll be taking your orders from him today."

Tyler tipped his hat in her direction. "Thank you, Miss Brooks."

She nodded in his direction. "As you all know, I've been back at the Bridal Falls for the last six months, and as you probably know, you haven't seen hide or hair of me, in the daylight anyway."

A ripple of no answers rose from the cowboys.

"That's because I was involved in a accident eight months ago that burned and scarred my face."

One by one J.P. eliminated each man based on the look of surprise in his expression.

"As you can see, I survived, but not without needing

skin grafts." She turned the left side of her face toward the group. "You don't see me out much in sunlight because it can upset the healing process of the grafts."

He watched her swallow hard and pull in a quick breath. The worst of it was over for her.

"Now to a more pressing matter, the assault on Devon Hall. Tyler can tell you he's doing fine and will be coming home tomorrow."

"Godspeed," Buck Walters said, nodding as the other members of the permanent crew chimed in with their own good wishes for the Bridal Falls foreman's return.

"Sheriff Adams is investigating the crime and has taken statements, but what you don't know is someone took potshots at J.P. Ryker and myself the same day while we were at Bridal Falls."

"You think it was the same nut job who clocked Devon?" Ruckus Bartlett asked as he pulled his cowboy hat off and rubbed his sleeve across his forehead before slapping it back on.

"Yes, and last night someone fired on the ranch truck Tyler was driving back from town. It's riddled with bullet holes."

"Damn," Buck said under his breath. "Why in the Sam Hill would someone want to hurt any of you?"

A blade of concern jittered across her nerves and knotted in her stomach. She'd managed to stir up more questions than answers. Now it was time to turn it over to J.P. before any information leaked out about the kidnapper's threats against her.

"That was precisely my question. And that's why I've hired J.P. to look after me."

On cue, he nudged his horse forward up next to hers. One by one her rigid muscles went slack.

"I was able to find a .308 shell casing in the woods

above the falls. It's been turned over to Sheriff Adams for his investigation. He's doing everything he can to find out who pulled the trigger, but it'd be helpful to Miss Brooks if you all kept an eye out for anything suspicious."

"You bet we will," Ruckus said, his sun-baked face lined and dead serious. "We can't have anyone shooting up the place."

The other cowpokes agreed.

"Then stay alert, stay safe and let's brand some cattle."

In a swirl of dust the crew disbanded, some toward the catch pens, others for the gate leading into the lower pasture next to the creek where a hundred head grazed.

"Thanks," she whispered in J.P.'s direction. "I almost took that revelation off into the weeds."

"You did a good job. If the guy responsible was listening, he's got to be concerned. I'd expect him to make a move soon."

A chill teased over her skin. "I'm going to shake out my horse."

"I'll get my assignment from Tyler."

Eve headed out into the field enjoying the feel of the sun on her shoulders. The sensation brought tears to her eyes. Free. She was finally free again. Her fear of seeing repugnance in the eyes of the crew had never materialized. A thrill zipped across her nerves and settled in her heart. She nudged Ginger with her heels.

The mare responded and lunged forward.

Caught off guard, she barely had time to lock her fingers around the saddle horn to keep her seat.

Pulling back on the reins with her right hand, she attempted to bring the horse under control.

Ginger bolted, shaking her head back and forth as she picked up speed.

"Whoa!" she hollered, attempting to get the animal's

attention, but it was too late. The agitated mare took the bit and dropped her head below her withers.

The reins jerked out of Eve's hand, and like a lasso, they snapped up and looped over the mare's head.

Fear cut a deep path through her insides as everything went to heck in a hurry.

The reins tangled with Ginger's ears. She spooked and took off across the field at a full gallop.

A scream ripped from Eve's throat as the berserk horse blasted past the holding pens and turned for the open field.

Grabbing on to the saddle horn with both hands, she squeezed so tight her fingers stung. Eve dropped forward, taking a low profile atop the out-of-control animal. If she could capture one of the reins, maybe she could stop the horse or gradually pull the mare into a circle.

Sliding her hand along Ginger's neck, she bent as far forward as she could and tried to grab hold of the rein on the left side, but she couldn't reach it.

Two seconds later, Ginger stepped on it, nearly sending the speeding horse to her knees before the leather snapped.

Terror pinned Eve to the saddle. She stared at the ground bucking and diving below her.

Could she bail off at this clip?

If she did, she risked breaking her neck.

The sound of thundering hoofbeats pounding the ground behind her brought her head around. She stared over her right shoulder for an instant, spotting J.P. three lengths behind her.

A cry rumbled in her throat, dislodged and died in the wind.

Glancing forward again, horror worked through her body and held the oxygen in her lungs. A hundred yards ahead was a rail fence, and beyond that, a dense stand of trees so thick she could barely see into them. Sudden death if she didn't get off this horse.

Now.

Spurring the big gelding, J.P. maneuvered to the left side of Eve's horse, watching their approach to the fence in slow motion.

Neck and neck, he pulled slightly ahead, reached out and grabbed hold of the broken rein slapping in the wind.

Guiding the gelding with a firm hand, he began a sweeping turn to the right, using the horse's body to block and steer Eve's mare away from the fence. Together they reached the top of the turn less than ten feet from the rails.

J.P. pulled hard on the single strap of leather, his only connection to the crazed mare and the woman on her back, but the horse refused to cooperate. With a toss of her head, she tried to jerk the rein from his hand.

Tightening his grip on the leather, he spurred the gelding slightly ahead.

What the hell was going on?

His suspicions were growing by the second. Only a drug could send a normally sound animal on a rampage like this. He had to get Eve off the horse, or risk having her mixed up in a final crash he knew was coming.

"Eve!"

She raised her head to stare at him from under the brim of her hat.

"Kick your feet out of the stirrups!"

Her eyes went large and round, her features dissolving into a mask of terror.

"I'm going to pull you off! Don't fight me!"

Her head bobbed in agreement, but the fear in her eyes remained as she slipped her booted feet out of the stirrups.

"Sit up!" he yelled against the wind.

She straightened in the saddle.

Urging his horse in as close as he could to the mare, he let go of the single rein, reached over and locked his arm around Eve's waist.

She went limp as he snagged her off the runaway horse.

Holding her like a rag doll, and counterbalancing in the saddle, he pulled back on the reins and brought the gelding to a stop.

He lowered her to her feet on the ground and dismounted next to her.

"Thank God you're okay." Wrapping his arms around her, he felt her tremble as she rested her head against his chest.

"I couldn't stop her once she took the bit." Pulling back, she turned to stare toward the corral, where the crew who'd witnessed the incident had managed to rope the mare and pull her inside.

"We better get the vet. I suspect she was drugged."

"What kind of maniac would do something like this?"

"Maybe the same nut who tried to keep Tyler's cow dog quiet the night he sabotaged the brakes on the SUV. Come on, let's get some help for your mare."

He climbed atop the gelding, then removed his foot from the stirrup so Eve could put hers in. Reaching down, he grabbed her hand and helped her swing on behind him.

"Thanks, Kemosabe," she whispered. "You've saved my butt again." She wrapped her arms around his chest, sending a shock wave ricocheting through his body. He wanted to breathe her in. Feel the sensation of her skin against his. Run his fingers over every inch of her exquisite body.

"Any time, Tonto." Reaching down, he put his hand over her clasped fingers and turned the horse toward the action transpiring in the corral.

Tyler and the crew had managed to get the saddle off the mare by the time they rode up and dismounted.

"I'm going to go cool him down." He nodded toward his horse, who was breathing hard and bathed in sweat.

"Okay." Eve turned and hurried to where Tyler was giving instructions to another crew member.

"Buck, go call the Hastings' ranch. They've got an equine vet up here from the valley for branding. We need him to come take a look at Miss Brooks's horse right away."

"Sure thing." Buck tipped his hat to her and sprinted for the lodge to make the call.

Eve went to the corral and stared through the railing at her horse, watching her buck like rough stock in a rodeo, then pause for a few moments before starting the cycle again. "J.P. says he thinks she's been drugged."

"That would be my guess, too. I tried to caution your dad about buying her from Grimes." Tyler turned to face her. "Rumor back then was he'd been doping his horses with fluphenazine."

"Fluphenazine?"

"It's used to enhance a horse's performance level, but some horses can have an allergic reaction to the drug. It can make them go berserk."

"But I've had her for years. That stuff would be out of her system by now. Unless…" A shudder hummed through her body. Unless the same person who had thrown the ransom note through the window last night also doped her horse, knowing she'd be riding her this morning.

"When the vet gets here, tell him what you suspect she may have been doped with. I'm going to let J.P. know." She turned and headed for the area next to the barn where he'd unsaddled and unbridled the bay. He was quick-cooling him now in a stream of water from the hose.

"How's she doing?" he asked, dropping the hose and moving over to shut off the valve.

"Not good. Tyler says Roger Grimes used to dope his

performance horses with a drug called fluphenazine. An allergic reaction can make them go nuts."

"You call the vet?" He began slicking the excess water off the horse's hide with a cupped aluminum spatula.

"Buck's doing it now. There's one a couple miles down the road working at another ranch."

"I'm sorry about your mare, but I'm glad you're okay." He studied her from under the brim of his dusty black Stetson.

"I could swear I saw the Lone Ranger charging after me when I glanced back."

"Really?" His expression was serious as he stared at her, but his clear blue eyes sparkled with amusement.

"Yeah." She smiled, feeling her worried mood lighten with the effort and the close proximity of her own knight in shining armor. "The only thing you need now is a white hat and a couple of six-guns. Oh, and a mask."

Eve glanced away at the sound of gravel crushing in the driveway, seeing a white pickup pull in, noting the veterinarian's medical box in the truck's bed liner. "There's the vet."

"Go. I'll find you as soon as I walk him out." J.P. stared after her, a degree of contentment stirring in his blood as he watched her walk away. Shoulders back, easy stride, head held high. She'd taken a huge step today. Her transformation couldn't be far from complete. She could come out of the shadows now, at least on the ranch, but L.A. was going to test her newfound confidence in ways that could tear her apart.

Worry battered his optimism. He wanted to be there for her, but she hadn't asked.

Turning back to his task, he finished slicking the water off the big bay's coat, pulled the lead rope free from the hitching post and led the horse away.

"GOTCHA." J.P. HELD UP a bullet, squeezed in the teeth of the pliers and dropped it into his palm. He'd lucked out and found it lodged in the tire he and Tyler had wrestled off the truck.

"With this slug—" he laid the tool on the work bench in the garage and stared at Tyler Spangler "—we can ballistically match it to the gun it was fired from."

"I never would have guessed you weren't a real cowpoke. You fooled the heck out of me this morning, chasing after Miss Brooks on that runaway horse. Are you a bodyguard?"

J.P. clamped his jaw tight against the urge to demand Tyler pay attention. Lives were at stake. "Miss Brooks doesn't feel safe right now. I'm here until she does."

"All right," Tyler said.

"I want you to play up this find at the barbecue in a few minutes. Tell anyone who will listen that we recovered a slug from the tire and plan to take it into Sheriff Adams in the morning so he can use it to identify the sniper."

"You think he'll show up here tonight?"

"I do. He knows this evidence can send him to prison for attempted murder. He's going to do whatever it takes to prevent me from delivering it to the authorities, including trying to mess with the vehicles."

"Be careful, J.P." Tyler turned and headed for the garage door. "I'll see you outside."

"Yeah," J.P. said as he trailed after Tyler and stepped out the side door. He paused for a minute to listen to the notes of guitar music as they drifted in from out on the front lawn where the barbecue was just beginning to sizzle. Eve's idea of rewarding her ranch crew for a hard day's work. He had to admit there wasn't a muscle in his body that wasn't screaming city slicker right now. The idea of a thick juicy steak, a beer and live music by a local artist sounded pretty good. Already the young woman's bluesy voice was pulling him in. Shoving the slug into his pocket, he reached back and locked the door behind him. If the saboteur wanted inside there tonight, he'd better be prepared for a fight.

Eve spotted J.P. coming out the door at the side of the garage and walked toward him.

"Hey, cowboy, how do you like your steak?"

"Medium rare."

"I'll let the grill master know, right after you tell me if you and Tyler found anything in the tire."

He shoved his hand into his pocket and produced the slug. "Found it on the inside of the tire. It was lodged in the sidewall. I'm taking it to Sheriff Adams in the morning."

Reaching out, she opened her hand. He dropped the bullet into her palm. "This could have done horrible damage if it had hit Spangler."

"Or anyone else, for that matter. Listen, Eve."

She handed it back and gazed up at him, noticing the way he scanned the group laughing and talking on the front lawn, just over her shoulder.

"I intend to use this slug as bait tonight. I'm going to need your help."

Pulling in a deep breath to combat the uneasiness sliding down her spine, she leaned closer. "What are you going to do? Hide it in the potato salad?"

He gave her half a grin. "No, I need you to bury it in the baked beans. Can you handle that, sweetheart?"

"I can do it." What she couldn't do was be this close to him without having her skin tingle and her body respond on a subconscious level.

J.P. leaned closer and whispered, "It won't hurt. I promise."

She saw him swallow hard, saw his pulse jump along

his carotid artery, saw the heat in his blue eyes. She wasn't the only one swimming against a riptide.

"Tell me what to do."

"Throughout the evening, I need you to mention the slug we found in the ranch truck's tire, and that I'm taking it to the sheriff in the morning so it can be matched to the .308 shell casing we found near the falls. My bet is the kidnapper or whoever is keeping him abreast is here tonight and listening. One way or another the information will get to him."

"That's it?"

"Yeah."

"You said it was bait." She studied him in the gathering twilight, working to pull the threads together. They intertwined in a net of apprehension that sprung inside her and trapped her nerves.

"No, J.P.! He's dangerous. The vet confirmed someone gave Ginger a dose of fluphenazine last night, knowing she'd go berserk this morning. He doesn't care about hurting anyone or anything. He's deadly. What if he shoots at you?"

"I'll shoot back."

"What if he doesn't miss this time?"

"Relax, Eve. I'll be prepared tonight, and if he doesn't come around here, he'll be waiting for me somewhere along the highway on my way into town tomorrow morning. I didn't just fall off the turnip truck. Trust me."

Stone-cold fear fanned out inside her chest, making it hard to breathe. She closed her eyes and pulled in a deep breath, then another, before she controlled the beginnings of a panic attack.

J.P. reached out and tipped her chin up with his fingers.

She opened her eyes to stare at him. His touch generated a hot spot near her heart.

"This is why you hired me, remember. To protect you, to get the SOB who's after you. We're so close. Let me do my job."

Caught in purgatory between yes and no, she could only find maybe in her heart. The thought of him being injured or killed bore a hollow place in her belly.

"You're the strategist. If you think it will draw him out into the open, I have to believe you're right." But she didn't have to like it. Knowing the man she was falling for might not survive.

She didn't like it one damn bit.

"Come on." She stepped back, regretting the disconnect as his hand fell away from her face. "There's still time to get your order in over at the grill. Dangerous confrontation, medium rare, with a helping of bravado on the side."

Sobering, she stared up at him, trying to read the look in his eyes, but she couldn't see through his wall of blue.

"Don't mind me." Irritation burned in her blood. All she could see was him injured and bleeding. Turning on her boot heels, she walked away. "Looks like I'm choking down a well-done worry, whether I like it or not."

Chapter Twelve

Eve was saucy....

Two seconds after she'd disarmed him at the BBQ with her witty repartee, he knew he'd never get enough of it as long as he lived. He wanted it 24/7. He wanted *her.* Indefinitely.

Readjusting his position at the northwest corner of the garage, he stared into the darkness, glad she was locked safely in her room upstairs right now, worrying about him.

She'd be more upset in the morning when he told her he couldn't allow her to come along on his trip into town. Perhaps her position would soften once he reminded her of the crash they'd survived the last time around.

Retraining his focus, he picked out Tyler's location in a bank of trees kitty-corner to the garage and homed in on his unmoving figure standing next to the trunk of a tall pine.

Night sounds assaulted his senses, buzzing around him in a frenzied hum of crickets and frogs. The creek gurgled and rushed past not one hundred yards from his location.

A flicker of movement in his peripheral sent a charge through his veins. Reaching up, he batted away a moth in search of a light source. But he'd made sure there were none tonight. Nothing to give away their presence in the dark. Waiting. Watching. Hoping to bring this to an end before anyone died.

He glanced at his watch. One a.m. on the dot. Around the same time the rock had come crashing through Eve's upstairs window.

Tension climbed his spine and kneaded the muscles between his shoulder blades. The situation was escalating. Was it too much to hope the thug had assumed a nocturnal high-time when he liked to roam the darkness and spread his brand of terror?

Caution roared in his eardrums as he strained to hear beyond the noise. There were only four ways into the three-bay garage, every one of them locked.

Somewhere beyond the bank of river willows and buck brush lining the edge of the stream, he saw something move.

His heart rate ticked up. Picking it out of the darkness, he watched a lone figure cross the driveway and blend into the brush. Had Tyler decided to move his location? Or was the kidnapper looking to make his move?

Pressing back into the shadows next to the side door of the garage, he pulled the .41 from its holster, stepped around the corner and worked his way along the front of the building. He'd intercept the thug when he stepped out of the willows, draw a bead on him and demand he stop in his tracks.

Pop!

J.P. heard the odd noise at the back of the garage, like a lightbulb imploding on a sidewalk. Recognition sliced across his brain.

Molotov cocktail?

He took off at a run headed for the back of the structure. Glancing up, he saw a yellow halo push into the night sky.

He rounded the end of the structure, raised his weapon and scanned the bank of trees for the attacker.

The echo of running footsteps across the wooden bridge over the creek changed his focus. Once the man who'd thrown the firebomb made it to the road, he'd never catch him.

Whoosh! The flames exploded, climbing up the back wall of the garage as they fed on the fuel.

"Tyler!" J.P. yelled, watching him materialize from his hiding place next to the tree, but he was headed in the wrong direction. "Tyler!"

Two seconds later, the clank of a cast-iron bell clapper shattered the night and sent out the alarm.

Pushing away from the cover of the structure, he ran down the driveway and across the bridge. Taking cover next to a pine, he stared into the darkness.

Nothing moved.

Listening, he tried to pick out the sound of footfalls or brush cracking. Nothing. The thug was probably hunkered down, determined to wait him out. That wasn't going to take much doing, since he couldn't see his hands in front of his face. He'd never seen night this black.

A rustle in the brush next to him brought his head around. He worked to pick out movement amongst the leaves, but it was the overwhelming smell that warned him he'd dared to step into someone else's territory.

It didn't take light for him to pick out the two brilliant white stripes running along the skunk's back.

Backing away slowly until he was out of the animal's firing range, he holstered his weapon, turned and ran back across the bridge.

The ranch crew had mobilized to save the garage.

Tyler and Buck were in the process of dragging a hose

line from the lodge, where it had been attached to a large water valve.

J.P. jumped in, grabbed the line and helped them drag it around to the back of the garage, where the fire had taken hold.

"Did you see who did this?" Tyler yelled over the roar of the flames.

"No. He took off across the bridge. He could have gone any direction."

Buck aimed the nozzle at the base of the flames and opened the valve. A high-pressure jet shot out of the hose. The flames hissed and died in the plume of water, and within a couple of minutes the fire was out.

"You guys have your own personal fire department?"

"Have to," Tyler said, "when the nearest fire truck is forty miles away. If we had to depend on them to put a fire out around here, this garage would be a pile of ash before they could get here."

"J.P.!"

J.P. turned at the sound of Eve's voice, watching her hurry across the driveway in her robe and a strategically placed scarf. She carried a flashlight, which she promptly shined in his eyes. "Is everyone okay!" In turn, she raked Tyler and Buck with the beam.

"Thanks to Tyler and Buck, the damage is minimal." He gestured to the black scorch pattern fanning out from its source of ignition, a Molotov cocktail.

"I need your light."

She handed it to him and he stepped closer to where the firebomb had smashed against the wall. Shining the beam onto the ground, he spotted the remains of the broken bottle. A beer bottle, judging by the brown glass scattered in the gravel.

Eve must have spotted it as well, because he heard her

quick intake of breath. "Someone started this fire on purpose, didn't they?" She turned to look at him.

"Yeah. I heard the bottle pop against the wall, but whoever threw it is long gone now."

"Did you get a look at him?"

"No. It was too dark. I never anticipated he'd do something like this." Worry ground over his nerves. It could just as easily have been the lodge, with Eve inside.

"Do you think—" she lowered her voice to a whisper "—it's the kidnapper?"

"Same hit-and-run tactic. It could be him."

One by one the towering yard lights snapped on as the rest of the crew put in an appearance in varying states of dress.

"Come on, let's get you back inside." He handed her the flashlight and turned to where Tyler was assigning duties in the mop-up phase.

"Troy and Cody, get a nail puller from the barn and pry up the siding. I want to make sure there's nothing hot inside the wall."

The brothers headed for the barn.

Tyler glanced up at them. "Night, Miss Brooks. We've got this situation under control."

"I'm sure you do, Tyler. Thanks."

J.P. escorted her across the driveway and around to the back door of the lodge, where they nearly collided with Edith.

"There you are, Miss Brooks. I just wanted to check on you and make sure you were okay."

"I'm fine, but the garage, not so much."

He studied Edith in the shadows of the porch light, noting the beads of sweat dotting her forehead. She looked frazzled, disjointed and upset, but he supposed being jolted out of bed at one-thirty in the morning by a fire alarm bell could produce those results. Still…

"Well, I'll head back to my cabin then. Good night."

"Good night."

J.P. nodded and waited for her to step past him before he took the steps behind Eve, aware of the lingering scent of starter fluid.

Edith Weber? The firebomber? Or had she simply helped her nephew Roger Grimes put the Molotov together?

"I'll take you upstairs, make sure everything's okay, then I'll take up watch from the front porch."

"Why? You don't think he'll come back tonight, do you?"

"I didn't think he'd try to burn the garage down, but he did. There's still plenty of time between now and dawn if he wants to make another attempt."

Concern worked over his nerves as he followed her up the stairs, anxious to have her tucked safely inside and out of harm's way. There were too many variables. Too many unknowns at work for him to let his guard down again and underestimate this adversary.

"You look beat, cowboy. How about some coffee?" Eve asked, holding the steaming mug out for J.P. to take.

"Sounds good, thanks." He took the cup from her.

She turned and sat down on the porch swing, pushed back her scarf and settled into the comfy cushions to watch the sun come up over the Bridal Falls. Life was good right now, even with everything going on. She owed that to J.P.

"Any more action last night after I went to bed?"

"No. It went quiet once Tyler and the crew turned in."

She wanted to say *good,* but the affirmation stuck in her throat. The firebomber's failure to try something else last night only meant he'd strike again. Her pulse rate ticked up as she gazed across at J.P.

"What time are we heading into town?"

"I'm leaving at nine." His eyes were fixed on her, intense pools of blue, deep and unyielding. Dangerous.

"I assume that means you want me to stay put while you go out looking for a confrontation?"

He sipped his coffee, once, twice. "It's too risky for you to be in the passenger seat, Eve. I think we both know that. Whatever he's willing to do to keep the bullet evidence from reaching Sheriff Adams, he's going to try on the trip into town. Have you forgotten that we damned near lost the SUV over the side of that mountain?"

Visions of gore too horrible to contemplate sprinted across her thoughts. "What can I do to help?"

Caught off guard, his stare softened a bit. "You can stay on the ranch today, surrounded by the branding crew. They're good men. They'll look out for you."

"Just promise me you'll come home in one piece." Her throat tightened almost to the point of pain. She swallowed against the tension and focused on J.P.'s handsome face. On the determined smile slowly arching the corners of his sexy mouth.

"It'll take more than this nut job to stop me."

"Speaking of nut jobs, I haven't had a chance to ask you if you'd consider coming back to Los Angeles with me for my meeting with Thomas." A knot squeezed in the pit of her stomach and wouldn't relent. She needed J.P. there for moral support when she gave Thomas the boot.

"I live in L.A., sweetheart. I've gotta go back sometime, to feed my goldfish, Fred. He hasn't eaten since I left."

"Of course you do." She grinned at him, amazed by his innate ability to take the edge off any subject with a slice of humor. The tension locked between her shoulder blades started to relent a degree at a time.

"Don't get me wrong, I do love it here." J.P. sobered, enjoying the serene set of her features. A beacon he planned to hang on to in the storm he knew would come.

"What's not to love?" he whispered, seeing her blossom in the streaks of sunlight piercing through the pines in dawn's wake. "Fresh air, open spaces, peace and quiet, no cell phone service."

And a determined kidnapper, who wanted to take what he'd realized he wanted.

Tipping his coffee mug, he drained the last of the java and stood up. "I need to get ready to go. Will you be okay out here?"

"My predicament is all your fault, you know."

"Really?" Curiosity melded with concern inside his head and sent a jolt of uneasiness charging through his limbs. Was it possible she'd discovered the information he'd withheld from her about her half sister? The confession he'd continually tamped down, knowing it would eventually resurface. Was this the day?

"I didn't have the guts to be sitting out here in broad daylight two weeks ago." She stared up at him, her fair blue eyes bright with the sheen of tears pooled on the rims.

Bone-deep desire brought him to his knees in front of her. If for any reason he didn't come home today, she had to know how beautiful she really was.

"You have all the courage you need, Eve."

Straying outside the bounds of his self-imposed restraint, he set his mug down and reached for her, cupping her face in his hands.

"It's always been inside you." Leaning in, he pressed his lips against her forehead, pulling in the scent of her hair, a mix of fresh air and roses.

Heat exploded inside him, rocking his nerves, burning her brand on his heart. He sucked it up and continued his leisurely seduction, all geared to imprint a message on her soul he hoped she'd never forget.

A moan slid up her throat.

Working strategically, he breathed her in as he kissed her cheek and trailed his lips down the right side of her slender neck.

She shuddered under his targeted assault, but went rigid the instant he switched it up to the other side and moved his mouth across the patch of scar tissue at the base of her neck.

A whisper of verbal protest started in her throat; he felt it vibrate across her vocal cords.

"Courage, Eve," he whispered, moving up to tease her earlobe before pressing a series of kisses across her battle-scarred cheek.

Intoxicated by the experience, he found her lips for an instant, then pulled back to look into her eyes before he lost all control.

"You're more beautiful now than you ever were. Don't let anyone make you think otherwise. Ever."

He snagged the empty mug and pushed to his feet, drained of any immunity he had against her. He couldn't risk getting caught in her sleepy blue gaze again, so without looking down, he walked to the front door of the lodge, pulled it open and went inside.

Eve remained glued to the seat of the porch swing long after she'd watched J.P. pull the Explorer out of the garage and take off down the driveway. Tyler Spangler wasn't far behind him in the ranch's truck, headed in to pick Devon up from the hospital and his dog, Hank, from the veterinarian.

J.P.'s words still echoed inside her head. Every place he'd applied his warm kisses on her skin still tingled with expectation. What would she do if he didn't come home?

Mustering the will, she shelved the disturbing thought, pushed up off the swing and headed inside to eat breakfast. There was plenty of work to do this morning to keep her mind occupied until he got home. Besides, worry was compound interest on trouble before it came due.

If anything happened to him, she'd simply hunt down the maniac responsible and show him how straight a country girl could really shoot.

J.P. ROLLED THROUGH the narrow pass, noting the elevation sign posted next to the highway at the summit, 8,230 feet. May as well be on top of the world. It sure felt like it, he decided, staring at the vista opening up in front of him. Rugged mountains as far as the eye could see. Too bad he didn't have time to pull over and take it all in.

Instead he scanned the sides of the road lined with buck brush and pine trees, working to pick out any place a would-be gunman could hide, but the possibilities were too numerous to count.

Frustrated, he glanced in the rearview mirror, dialing in Tyler Spangler's position three car lengths back.

A degree of tension loosened its hold on his muscles. At least he'd have backup if the kidnapper made a move to recover the slug he had in his possession.

J.P. eased into the first sweeping S-turn and feathered his brakes, remembering the sickening sensation that had frayed his nerves the last time he'd taken this ride over the summit.

Glancing up into the mirror, he noticed Tyler had closed the distance between their vehicles. Understandable. Spangler had undoubtably made this trip so many times he knew every turn, every nuance in the strand of asphalt winding down off the mountainside.

Wham!

J.P. slammed forward in the driver's seat, his seat belt cutting a band across his chest.

"What the hell!" He glanced in the side mirror, spotting the ranch truck less than two feet from his rear bumper.

Was it possible the thug had somehow gotten to the brakes on the truck last night? If so, was the Explorer capable of stopping them both?

The roar of the truck's diesel engine filled the interior of the Explorer, its volume increasing with every passing second.

Caution surged in his blood.

Wham! Another hit.

He jolted forward, his eyes locked on the sweeping turn up ahead. The same corner where he'd driven the SUV into the mountainside to avoid the hairpin turns below.

A flash in the side mirror caught his attention.

Tyler nosed the truck out from behind the Explorer and into the oncoming lane.

In a burst of speed, the truck shot alongside the Explorer.

Realization ground through him, making dust out of his false perceptions.

There wasn't anything wrong with the ranch truck's brakes; it was the driver behind the wheel.

Neck and neck the two vehicles skidded into the corner.

He slammed on his brakes to avoid the sideswipe, but Tyler deliberately steered the truck into the side of the Explorer.

Crunch! Metal on metal.

Hands locked on the steering wheel, J.P. fought to keep

the vehicle on the road, watching the edge of the highway drop off on his right.

Eve's attacker had been on the ranch the whole time. How in the hell had he missed all the signs?

Anger stirred inside him, brewing renewed determination.

The truck was longer and heavier than the Explorer, but he didn't plan on dying today and leaving Eve vulnerable to the likes of Tyler Spangler.

Yanking the wheel to the left, he shoved the truck over as they pulled out of the turn and into a short, straight stretch.

Dead ahead, yellow caution signs blazed a warning into his brain, pegging the upcoming hairpin turn at twenty-five mph.

J.P. gritted his teeth, dissecting Spangler's plan as the seconds ticked by. Tyler would try to force the Explorer off the corner from the left-hand lane and send it, and him, rolling down the mountainside onto the switchback below. If the crash didn't kill him, then Spangler would probably attempt to finish the job.

Against his instincts, he forced the accelerator to the floor, shot past the truck and straddled the center line, praying he didn't meet any oncoming traffic.

Checking his rearview mirror, he watched the truck accelerate behind him.

Squeezing the steering wheel, he maneuvered to the left, blocking Tyler's attempt to pull alongside.

Crunch!

The Explorer shuddered.

Tyler swerved to the right, making another attempt to get around him.

J.P. cranked the wheel to the right and blocked the pass.

His tires squealed as he rocketed past the warning signs

and accelerated into the hairpin turn, shifting the vehicle's weight and sucking it to the road.

Pulling the steering wheel hard to the left, he forced the Explorer into the oncoming lane and jammed the brakes.

The truck shot past him on the right at the apex of the turn.

In his peripheral he saw the truck's brake lights flare, but it was already too late.

Tyler Spangler had overshot the corner.

Truck and driver disappeared over the edge.

Chapter Thirteen

J.P. steered the Explorer onto the thick left shoulder of the road and slid to a stop on the loose gravel.

He popped his seat belt, hit the emergency flashers and bailed out of the rig. Racing across the highway, he hurried to the edge and looked over, spotting the mangled remains of the truck two hundred feet below, where it had come to rest in a tangle of twisted metal. Its path of rapid descent was evidenced by the destruction of vegetation in its path, save the ancient pine it now rested against.

Caution surged through him as he watched for anything moving below. If Spangler had survived the crash it would be a miracle, but he had to find out for himself.

The sound of a car engine turned his attention to the highway.

An older couple in a red car with out-of-state plates slowed and pulled onto the side of the road in front of him. The flashers came on, the driver's side door opened and a man climbed out.

"Is everything okay?" he asked as he stepped up next to J.P. to stare over the edge of the embankment.

"No."

"What happen— Is that a truck?"

"Yeah. He just blew off the corner. I'm going down

to see if the driver is alive. I need you to find the nearest phone and call 911."

"We just came from the Wapiti Meadow guest ranch. We'll head back and make the call."

"Thanks." He waved a send-off to the man, whose pallor was a shade grayer by the time he turned and hurried for his car. He climbed in, flipped a U-turn on the highway and roared off in the same direction he'd come. Some folks just didn't have the stomach for gore. This good Samaritan was probably one of them.

Sobering, he started his descent over the steep embankment, grabbing hold of brush and saplings as he tried to keep from careening head-first down the mountainside.

Glass and debris littered the impact zone. Shattered and scattered bits of the truck's taillights and windows. Hunks of the right front quarter panel.

The smell of raw fuel invaded his nostrils ten feet from the wreckage. Thank God the truck was diesel and not gasoline, or he'd be staring into an inferno right now. He stumbled forward, went to his knees and looked inside the crushed cab of the truck through what had been the passenger side window frame.

Empty.

Agitated, he pushed to his feet and turned slowly around to stare up the incline. The hairs on the back of his neck bristled.

"Spangler! Where are you? Can you hear me?"

The decisive click of a hammer being pulled back on a pistol focused his attention on the right side of the debris field twenty feet from where he stood.

"You need help, Tyler."

He never should have come down here unarmed.

"Blowing a hole in me isn't going to save you. Let me help." He took several steps up the mountainside.

"Tell me how it went down. You figured since you couldn't collect the ransom the first time around, you'd try again?"

Five more steps and he caught the sound of Spangler's labored inhales and exhales, like a dying man's last grasp on life.

"Eve's not going to pay the ransom. She told me so when she hired me to catch the kidnapper harassing her."

His eyes picked out Tyler's prone outline in a patch of field grass growing up from a cross-lay of dead trees.

"You're wasting your time, Spangler."

"The…hell…I am." Tyler's voice was weak, barely above a whisper. "Said we'd…split the money three ways if we made her…pay."

"Who, Tyler?" Panic sparked across his nerves. He took another couple of steps toward Spangler, determined to extract as much information as he could, but the cocked pistol in Tyler's hand kept him from charging in.

"Tell me who's running the show. Is it Grimes?"

"He's…dead."

"Roger Grimes is dead? How do you know that?" One more step and he could clearly see Tyler Spangler lying on the ground. A knot formed in his stomach as he stared at the spiny branch sticking up out of the middle of Spangler's chest. He'd been thrown clear of the wreckage and impaled in the process.

"Did you kill him?"

Spangler's head rolled to the right.

Their stares locked for an instant before Tyler's arm went slack at the elbow. He exhaled his dying breath with the pistol squeezed in his hand, his finger on the trigger. It hit the ground next to him.

A shot fired out of the gun.

J.P. hit the dirt, feeling a sudden sting. Hot and wet,

the bullet burned across his right cheekbone and drilled into the ground next to him, sending up a puff of dust that clouded his vision.

Relief surged in his veins, dropping his adrenaline level like a rock. Rolling over onto his back, he rubbed the grit out of his eyes and stared up at the sky.

An inch to the left and he'd be missing parts, namely the back of his skull. Then what would Eve do? Hell, what would he do?

Holding up his arm, he noted the time on his watch. A quarter to ten. It would be a while before help arrived, then there would be paperwork and reports and questions.

He closed his eyes and envisioned Eve's face in his mind's eye.

"J.P. RYKER?" SHERIFF ADAMS'S gravelly voice drilled into his brain. "You okay?"

Squinting against the sun, he opened his eyes to stare up at the sheriff and two of his deputies. Reaching up, he touched the swath of flesh on his right cheek. The action made him wince. He pulled back bloodied fingers.

"Just great, Sheriff." He must have dozed off.

Raising up onto his elbows, he tried to get his bearings. One look at the wrecked truck directly in front of him, and orientation was over. He pushed up into a sitting position, then climbed to his feet and dusted himself off.

"Did you find Tyler Spangler's body over there?" He nodded to where he lay lifeless.

"Yeah. Want to tell me what happened here?"

"He tried to run me off the road. Almost succeeded, but took the plunge instead. I came down to see if he was still alive, and he pointed a pistol at me. Admitted he's been trying to collect the botched ransom money from Miss Brooks. When I pressed him about Roger Grimes's involvement in the scheme, he told me Grimes was dead. His dying act was to involuntarily fire a round that grazed my cheek."

"He's telling the truth, Sheriff," one of the deputies said as he knelt next to Spangler's body and stared at the position of the weapon. "Tyler's still got the pistol gripped in his hand with the trigger compressed."

"Spangler said Grimes was dead?" The sheriff studied him from under the brim of his hat.

"Yeah. I asked him if he killed him, but by then he wasn't talking anymore."

J.P. glanced down at his watch. "What the heck?" Ten o'clock? He tapped his watch with his knuckle to make sure it was working.

"You got the time, Sheriff?"

"Yeah." He raised his wrist. "It's ten."

"How'd you get here so quick? There's no way you're responding to this accident." Realization hummed through his body. "You're headed for the Clayton Ranch?"

"Yes. A call came in around eight a.m. from Edith Weber. She said she discovered her nephew Roger Grimes dead in his home from a self-inflicted gunshot wound."

"Damn." The air locked in his lungs. "Spangler knew Grimes was dead this morning, either because he stopped by and discovered the body, or because he fired the fatal shot. They were in on this together."

"It's possible, but I have to let the evidence tell me the story, Mr. Ryker."

"I wouldn't want it any other way, Sheriff." J.P. dug into his pants pocket and pulled out the slug. "This is the bullet we took out of one of the tires from that truck after someone fired on it. I think your forensic team will determine it came from a .308 and will match the shell casing I gave you."

J.P. handed the slug to Sheriff Adams.

"Well, I'll be. Looks like .308 ammo."

"I phoned the report in to your office yesterday morning."

"I saw the report. How's Miss Brooks holding up under the threat of the ransom note?"

"She's scared, but determined. I think it was Grimes, or Spangler for that matter, according to what he said. They're in on this scheme together."

"Trying to get Miss Brooks to pay the ransom?" Sheriff Adams asked as he handed the bullet to his deputy, who put it into an evidence bag.

"Makes sense. Everything that has happened at the Bridal Falls Ranch up to this point has been geared to scare her into paying the money." Caution worked through his body and set his thoughts on Tyler Spangler's dying confession. He'd admitted he and someone else, presumably Roger Grimes, were trying to make Eve pay the ransom, so they could split it. He recalled the statement from Tyler word for word. He'd said they'd split the money three ways if we made her pay.

We? Who was *we* in the scenario? Presumably, Spangler and Grimes. If so, who was the third person involved?

"Mind if I tag along with you to the Clayton Ranch?"

"Nope. Matter of fact, I was going to ask you to come. I can always use another set of professional eyes. Officer Richards can take your accident statement while we're there."

J.P. nodded, and stared up the imposing length of the mountainside. He was less than enthusiastic about the climb out of here, but at least he'd be doing it on his own two feet and not in a body bag.

"I'm going to start the climb, Sheriff." Without looking back, he took off up the steep hillside and headed for the top, more concerned about Eve's safety now than he'd ever been. Until he knew who else was involved, he had to remain vigilant.

J.P. MADE HIS THIRD TRIP around Roger Grimes's lifeless body, which sat upright in a dining-room chair. The shotgun had been propped in a homemade stand before the percussion from the blast had propelled it onto the floor at the far end of the table. Something was hinky. He just didn't know what yet.

Leaning closer, he studied the stippling on Grimes's neck. Tiny black dots where hot gunpowder had peppered his skin.

"Sheriff, I think I found something."

"What is it, Ryker?" Sheriff Adams moved closer, aiming his miniflashlight where J.P. pointed.

"Right there. Do you see those two small red marks an inch apart?"

"Yeah."

"Taser burns. I've seen them dozens of times on kidnapped victims. The attacker uses the Taser to subdue them before he restrains them. It's quiet and gives him control instantly. No chance the victim is going to escape."

"Good work."

"Thanks."

"As soon as the coroner arrives, we can get a time of death, see if it lines up with your theory Tyler Spangler may have killed Grimes."

"Looks like he's the one who fired on Eve and I at the falls."

"You're sure?"

"Check out his left hand."

Sheriff Adams bent slightly to examine Grimes's bandaged hand. "You said you thought Miss Brooks winged him. You were right."

J.P. nodded, then turned his attention to the interior of Grimes's place, looking for anything that caught his eye. He stepped into the kitchen, noting a cubby area next to the telephone where a brown paper bag had one side missing. It had been cut apart with a pair of scissors still lying on top of what remained of the bag, and next to it was a pile of scrap magazine ads and newspaper clippings.

"There's more in here."

Sheriff Adams stepped into the kitchen. "What's the significance? It looks like an art project."

"Or the place where Grimes constructed the ransom note wrapped around the rock that came through Eve Brooks's window. It was cobbled together using scrap letters, like these."

"Do you still have it?"

"No, I had Edith Weber mail it out to the lab for me, but it looks like it'll come back clean." He pointed to a pair of discarded rubber gloves lying next to a bottle of glue. "My guess is Grimes had sense enough to wear those."

He studied the sheriff for a moment. "Grimes was in this ransom scheme up to his eyeballs, along with Tyler, but there's someone else involved who's still out there. We need to find them quickly before they can harm Eve Brooks."

"I agree. I'll call in some backup and we'll head for the Bridal Falls. Maybe a search of Tyler's place will turn up more evidence."

"Yeah. Mind if I keep looking?"

Adams nodded. "Go right ahead."

"Thanks." J.P. moved through the rest of the house room by room with a knot in his stomach. Grimes appeared to be like anyone else around here, decent, hardworking. So what had turned him into a criminal? What had taken Tyler down the same damn path? He didn't know for certain, but he planned to find out.

He returned to the living room as Officer Richards came in from the garage. "I found a .308, Sheriff, along with a handful of other weapons."

"Any chance you saw a Glock 9 mm out there with the initials JPR on it and a computer hard drive?"

"As a matter of fact, I did."

"Belong to you, Ryker?" the sheriff asked.

"Yeah, stolen the first night I spent at the Bridal Falls, along with my computer's hard drive. I didn't report it at the time, because I'd just arrived undercover at the ranch and didn't want to draw attention to myself."

"So odds are, Grimes knew who you were from the moment you stepped foot on the ranch."

"Could be." Irritation spread through him like wildfire. He should have hit the ground in attack mode, never let the theft happen.

"Don't sweat it. There isn't much that goes on in these parts that someone isn't privy to. As soon as we get the scene processed, we'll release those items back to you."

"I'd appreciate that." He needed fresh air and time to think. "Excuse me." Stepping past Deputy Richards, he walked out the open front door of the house and paused on the porch to stare out over the landscape. He was fairly certain Tyler Spangler had murdered Roger Grimes and tried to cover it up by making it appear to be a suicide, but what had precipitated it?

The clatter of shoed hoofbeats thundered at the base of the long driveway up to the house.

Squinting against the sun, he spotted a horse and rider galloping out of the trees lining the drive.

It was Eve.

Concern hitched to his nerves. Edith had probably told her about Grimes, but it didn't explain why she was here and not back at the safety of the ranch.

He took the wide steps down off the porch, his muscles cranking tighter between his shoulder blades with every step. He would have to tell her about Tyler Spangler's death and his admitted connection to the threats and harassment. It was going to be a bitter pill for her to swallow. He knew how much she liked the easygoing cowpoke. Hell, he'd liked him, too.

Eve reined Ginger in and trotted past the Explorer, or what was left of it. The rear end was smashed in along with the entire passenger side of the vehicle from nose to tail.

"Whoa." She pulled back on the reins and stopped her horse at a hitching post just below the house. Glancing up, she caught sight of J.P. as he headed toward her.

Grim was the only thought that popped into her head. His expression was really grim.

Looping the reins around the post, she stepped around her horse and met him in the middle of the drive.

Her heart rate ticked up when they came face-to-face and she saw the bloody streak cut across his right cheek.

"My gosh, J.P., what happened?" Reaching up, she stroked her fingertips along his jawline for an instant. "You've been in an accident!"

Reaching out, he caught both of her wrists and pulled her against him. "Eve. Tyler Spangler's dead."

"What!" Her knees went weak, but J.P. held her up. "No." Tears burned behind her eyelids, along with flash memories of Spangler's helpful nature and slow grin. "How?"

"He tried to force me off the road at the hairpin turns this morning. He went over the edge and rolled the truck. He died at the scene."

She leaned into him. He released her wrists and wrapped his arms around her. She closed her eyes for a moment, processing the sad details, then pushed back to stare up at J.P.

"Wait a minute, Tyler tried to run you off the highway?"

"Yeah."

"Why would he do that? Unless—"

"He was involved in the kidnapping scheme to get you to pay the ransom money."

Her heart squeezed inside her chest as the venom of that knowledge flowed through her veins. Someone she'd trusted had betrayed her again.

"Why are you here with the sheriff?"

"Edith didn't tell you?"

"I gave Edith the day off. I haven't seen her since early this morning. I only knew you were here because I saw the Explorer from the lower southwest pasture, where Ruckus and I were chasing cows."

"Roger Grimes is dead, too."

"I need to sit down." Turning, she headed for the bottom step of the porch. "What happened to him?"

"Edith called it in to 911 this morning, according to Sheriff Adams. It looked like a suicide on first glance, but Grimes has Taser burns on his neck. Someone disabled him, then shot him."

"That's horrible." A wave of nausea roiled in her belly. "Is he…was he a part of this?"

"Looks that way. There's evidence he put together the ransom demand note that came through your window the other night. We found his .308, and my missing Glock and hard drive. Grimes and Spangler were both involved, to what extent and who did what, we may never know for certain."

"How could I have been so clueless?" Frustration bubbled inside her.

"Don't beat yourself up. I didn't peg Tyler for this either, and I'm a security expert."

She took some comfort in J.P.'s humble admission, but two people were still dead and they weren't coming back.

Sheriff Adams's boot falls against the floorboards of the porch brought J.P.'s head around.

Eve reached up and casually brushed her hand across the pressure dressing she'd applied over her scars this morning.

"Miss Brooks?"

"Yes."

Reaching down, J.P. caught hold of Eve's hand and helped her to her feet.

"I assume Mr. Ryker just told you about your ranch hand Tyler Spangler."

Eve turned to look up at the sheriff. "Yes."

"I'd like to search Spangler's bunkhouse for evidence. Since he's deceased, and the room is on your property, you can give us permission in lieu of a warrant."

"Yeah. Sure, anything I can do to help."

"Thank you. We'll be over as soon as we're finished here and the coroner arrives."

J.P. waited until Sheriff Adams had gone back inside before he grasped Eve's upper arms and turned her to face him. "There's something I need you to do."

"Doctor your cheek? It looks bad, J.P. It's going to leave a mark."

He shook his head. "Can you tell me who else knows exactly what the kidnapper's note said?"

She shuddered, a tiny quake of fear vibrating underneath his grasp. "Edith does. I showed her the note Thomas's kidnapper put under the windshield wiper of my car in L.A. She also took one of the ransom calls."

Eve swayed on her feet.

J.P. reached out and locked his arms around her to keep her upright. "I've got you, sweetheart."

"You think Edith is involved?"

"Yeah. It makes sense. You said you gave her the day off?"

"I did."

"Is she at the ranch right now?"

"No. I didn't see her car."

"Come on, let's get you out of here." He shuttled her to the hitching post, where he pulled her against him. "I'll get to the bottom of this, Eve. I promise." A surge of caution skimmed across his nerves and settled in his gut.

"I won't let anyone hurt you again."

Chapter Fourteen

Eve soaked the cotton ball in hydrogen peroxide and dabbed at the wound on J.P.'s cheekbone. It didn't take a medical degree to realize how close he'd come to being killed if the bullet had taken a steeper angle.

"How bad was the accident?" she asked, not sure she really wanted to know.

"Bad enough." He reached out and stroked his finger along her arm, almost making her drop the bottle.

"Suffice it to say, I'm glad you weren't in the passenger seat."

"Me, too." She finished cleaning the wound and smoothed antibiotic cream on it with a swab. "So it's over, right? Just tell me it's finally over."

"I can't. You know that." He sat on the edge of the sofa. "Until we can positively identify the third person involved, it's not finished."

"I was afraid you'd say that."

"Don't let it get to you." He pushed forward and stood up.

"Okay." She came to her feet in front of him.

"The sheriff and his deputy rolled up the driveway five minutes ago. I'd like to be there when they search Tyler's bunkhouse."

Eve nodded, thankful she had him to rely on. "J.P.?"

"Yeah."

"I'm glad you're safe. I don't know what I would do if you'd have been the one who didn't make it this morning."

He reached out and stroked his finger along her jaw, raised her chin, and lowered his lips to hers.

Desire, ancient and sweet, took hold in her limbs. She was breathless when he ended the kiss.

"I'll see ya in a bit. Lock the door and stay inside."

"Okay." She followed him to her studio door and watched him walk down the hallway, listening to the solid thud of his boots on the wood floor. Reaching into her jeans pocket, she took out her key, closed the door and slipped it into the lock. Turning back into the interior of the studio, her knees quivered as she collapsed on the sofa and tried to regain her equilibrium.

J.P. HEADED FOR BUNK ROW with the feel of her kiss still on his mouth. Training his focus, he stared at the sheriff's vehicle parked in front of Tyler's bunkhouse and gritted his teeth. He took the steps and stood outside on the porch while Sheriff Adams and Deputy Richards searched the place.

"Ryker?"

"Yeah."

"Come on in here, take a look around."

He stepped through the open door into the bunk room, where Sheriff Adams stood with his hands on his hips. "The place looks clean. Not so much as a weapon. You see anything here we might have missed?"

Glancing around the room, he noticed a small glass vial sitting on the nightstand. "May I?" He motioned to the table next to the bed. "Somebody drugged Eve's horse with fluphenazine. I'd assumed it was Grimes."

"Go ahead."

J.P. walked over and knelt beside the nightstand to read the label on the vial. "It's fluphenazine. Looks like Grimes wasn't the one who used this stuff to make Eve's horse go berserk. It was Spangler." He wondered what else the trusted ranch hand had done behind the scenes. He pushed to his feet.

"Sheriff, you better take a look at this," the deputy said as he pulled a large baggie out of the refrigerator and held it up.

J.P. stared at the missing hunting knife and sketch pad. "Damn. That's the evidence that went missing from my saddlebag."

"Looks like Tyler Spangler was heavily involved," Sheriff Adams said. "Book it into evidence along with the vial. I'm assuming Miss Brooks's horse made a full recovery?"

"Yes, she did. Thanks to a vet just up the road at another ranch."

"Glad to hear it."

"If we're done here, I'm going to head for the lodge. I'll be there if you need anything."

"Thanks, Ryker." Sheriff Adams extended his hand and he shook it. "Richards, give Ryker his Glock and hard drive."

The deputy picked up both items from the counter and handed them to him.

"I appreciate it." He released the clip and checked the weapon over. It was ready to fire. Clipping the holster on his belt, he picked up the computer hard drive from the counter and turned to leave.

"You've been a tremendous help with this investigation. If you ever decide to settle in these parts and need a position, come see me."

J.P. nodded. "I'll keep that in mind." Anxious to check

on Eve, he headed out the door, realizing for one moment he'd actually considered the sheriff's offer.

EVE PULLED A COUPLE MORE tissues from the box on the coffee table and held them out to Edith. "I'm sorry you had to find him like that. Maybe you should consult with a grief counselor about what you saw. It might make you feel better."

Edith Weber dabbed her eyes and blew her nose. "Maybe I will, after my sister and her husband arrive to make the funeral arrangements."

She was sorry for the woman's loss, but there would be no more attacks on the Bridal Falls Ranch now that the two men were dead. Curiosity glided over her thoughts as she studied Edith, wondering what role, if any, the woman had played in Roger and Tyler's scheme. They'd gotten their information from somewhere.

"Edith, I know this might not be the best time, but I need to ask you a few questions." She squared her shoulders, wondering if she should wait for J.P. to put in an appearance before she questioned her. But she wanted to handle it. After all, Edith was her employee, and she had an obligation to mete out any redress necessary.

"Certainly, Miss Brooks."

"I never told you exactly why I hired Mr. Ryker."

"No, you didn't."

"I hired him specifically in response to the threatening phone calls I received almost a month ago."

"I remember."

"J.P. and Sheriff Adams have discovered evidence Roger Grimes and Tyler Spangler were in on a scheme together to try and scare me into paying the ransom the kidnapper wasn't able to collect after Thomas was taken."

Edith's demeanor changed. She crossed her arms over

her chest and sank low in the sofa cushions. "Are you try-ing to accuse me of something, Miss Brooks?"

Eve sucked in a deep breath, noting the waterworks that seemed to flow so freely from Edith's eyes a moment ago had dried up like a desert.

"Someone on this ranch fed them information. Where I planned to go, when I'd be there and the precise demands the kidnapper made. You heard one of the calls verbatim. I showed you Thomas's ransom note. You're the only person I gave access to my schedule. I confided elements of my past to you, as well. Things no one else on the ranch knew."

Realization collided with horror in her brain. She men-tally picked through the information she'd shared with Edith Weber in the past few months. Things about her accident, and Thomas's kidnapping. The botched ransom drop. She stared at Edith, watching her eyes narrow to slits.

"I think it's time for me to go, Miss Brooks."

Caution seized her nerves. Her attention focused on the woman she thought she knew, as she pushed to her feet and snagged her purse from the coffee table.

"Save your breath if you're going to fire me, because I quit!"

She held her retort, sensing Edith's anger coalescing in the vibe of the room. Where was J.P.? He should be back by now. She should have waited for him before she raised questions.

Edith's footfalls hammered against the hardwood floor. She rounded the end of the sofa, her face pinched with hatred. "I'll have my things cleared out of the cabin this afternoon."

A chill sliced across the back of her neck. Every fiber in her body screamed in warning. She looked back over her right shoulder in time to see Edith pull something from her purse.

Rocking forward on the sofa, she tried to avoid the prongs of the Taser as Edith jammed it against the side of her neck. But she wasn't fast enough.

Edith pressed the button.

A jolt sizzled through her. Her teeth clenched. Every muscle went rigid. Mind-bending pain streaked through her body on a supersonic trip.

Falling, she was falling. Unable to stop herself, she collapsed on the floor next to the sofa.

In two seconds Edith was rolling her over.

Stunned, she stared up at the ceiling, unable to move. Unable to fight the things going on around her.

A scream gurgled in her throat. Her tongue was thick, unresponsive.

"Why couldn't you just have paid the ransom! It's not like you don't have it. Now I'm going to have to hurt you if someone doesn't pay."

Eve blinked as she watched Edith dig in her purse and produce a roll of duct tape. She tore off a strip.

"We were going to split it three ways. Do you know what we could have done with that kind of money?" Edith fingered the tape, grabbed it with an end in each hand and forced it down on Eve's mouth.

"When that kidnapper's call came in I saw my chance, and it would have worked too, but you hired Ryker to snoop around. I knew he was trouble the minute he climbed out of the helicopter. Roger got nervous, said he was going to the sheriff. What an idiot. I couldn't let him ruin everything."

Horror pulsed in her veins as the weight of Edith's admission crushed her resolve. Everything that had happened on the ranch was the result of a plot Edith had conceived after taking the real kidnapper's call. She could find it brilliant if it wasn't so terrifying.

Edith reached down, jerked the silk scarf off Eve's neck

and rolled her over onto her stomach. She wrapped the scarf around her wrists and yanked it tight.

"I can't carry you out. You're going to have to walk. The crew is busy branding, Ryker is with the sheriff going through Tyler's cabin and Charleen is taking a nap."

Edith let out a grunt as she pulled her up into a sitting position against the sofa, stood up and went into the galley kitchen.

She came back with a butcher knife. "If you give me any trouble, I'll use this on the pretty side of your face and cut you to ribbons. I swear I will."

Eve blinked, taking in the determined set of Edith's mouth, the desperation in her voice. She was desperate, and desperate people did desperate things. How could she have been so gullible? The woman she'd once believed was sweet and helpful, a confidante, was waving a blade in her face.

J.P., where are you?

"Wake up, Blondie." Edith reached out and squeezed a bare patch of skin on her upper arm.

Pain radiated from the vicious pinch.

She jerked away.

A glimmer of satisfaction flared in Edith's dark eyes. "Time to go."

Eve struggled to her feet without the use of her arms, relying on Edith, who pulled and worked to help her stand upright, but always with the butcher knife close to her body.

Panic ignited in Eve's veins when they reached the landing. She stared down into the stairwell, praying J.P. chose that moment to open the door and rescue her, but he didn't.

Two minutes later they were on the threshold. Fear carved a mark on her heart as she stared at Edith's car parked ten steps from the back door of the lodge.

The trunk lid was open. Waiting for her like the jaws of a great white. She would have only one chance to escape.

"Don't get any ideas," Edith said from next to her. "I'll drop you where you stand."

She thrust the tip of the knife. It pricked her in the ribs, a gentle slip of the blade meant to terrify. It worked, as rivulets of blood trickled from the wound, tickling the skin inside her blouse.

Eve sucked in a breath, focusing on the steps to the car. *Four... Three... Two... There.*

In a last-chance move, Eve lunged forward between Edith and the open trunk.

A crack on the back of her head forced spots up in front of her eyes. Dizzy from the blow, she lost her balance at the same time Edith steered her head-first into the trunk of the Buick.

She hit with a violent thud, then felt her legs being bent and folded into the compartment.

Rage shot through her, stirring her blood with strength she didn't know she had.

"Grrr," she screamed against the duct tape. Kicking her left leg back, she made contact with Edith's body.

"Stop!"

Never.

She kicked again, this time finding only air.

Switching up the angle, she shoved with her right leg and caught Edith again.

"Bitch!"

Legs together, she thrust her feet out as hard as she could.

Zap.

The prongs of the Taser bit into her leg just above her kneecap.

Muscles clenched, her face ground into the lining of the trunk.

Air.

She couldn't breathe.

Relief surged in her veins the moment Edith reached in, grabbed her by the arms and rolled her over onto her back.

"Should have let you suffocate. But you're no good to me dead." Grabbing her legs where they poked out of the trunk, she wrestled them into the compartment.

Edith's angry expression disappeared as the trunk lid slowly came down.

Mustering all the energy she had left, Eve raised her right leg and pressed her calf parallel to the opening. The lower leg of her pants tightened, catching between the lip and trunk lid.

She closed her eyes, listening to the car door shut. The engine fired up, and she prayed J.P. would see the sliver of fabric hanging out of Edith's car as she drove away.

The fleeting image of Shelly's final moments on earth lodged in her brain. Shelly had been asphyxiated at the hands of her kidnapper.

Horror knotted her stomach. She screamed into the tape. With her left foot she kicked the right side of the trunk with all the force she could coax from her noncompliant body.

Then she did it again and again and again.

TENSION CHURNED IN J.P.'s bloodstream as he hurried for the lodge and Eve, unsure why an overwhelming sense of urgency spurred him forward.

Glancing up, he spotted Edith's maroon Buick as she pulled away from the back door of the lodge and eased her car around the circular drive that would take her off the ranch.

What was she doing here?

Stopping in the middle of the drive, he waited for her to maneuver around the top of the loop past the front of the barn, before he raised his hands and waved to flag her down.

The car lurched forward.

He heard the throaty rev of the engine along with a thud coming from the rear of the car. Then another one. The trunk?

"Stop!" he ordered.

Edith accelerated, aiming straight for him.

At the last second, he bolted for the edge of the driveway.

The car shot past.

He broke into a run, spotting a slice of clothing trapped in the trunk lid of Edith's car.

"Eve!" Adrenaline shot through him, supercharging his legs. Sprinting across the side yard next to the lodge, he aimed for the bridge across the creek, the narrowest point Edith would have to steer the car through.

Edith Weber had to be the third person in the kidnapping plot. He could never let her make it across, or Eve was a goner.

Flipping the snap on his side holster as he ran, he drew the Glock. Jolting to a stop, he took a stand in front of the bridge entrance and raised his weapon.

Edith accelerated past the garage.

Aiming high on the windshield of the passenger side, he squeezed off two rounds.

Pop! Pop!

She kept coming.

Pop! Pop!

Squeezing off two more rounds, he put them through the grill into the radiator.

She kept coming.

J.P. took aim.

Time clicked by at a slow-mo crawl.

He pulled the trigger and saw Edith flinch over the top of the gun sight.

The car veered off the left side of the drive and plowed into the bank of trees next to the creek. Limbs cracked, pine needles rained, the horn blared.

Caution infused his body. He lunged for the wreckage with his weapon raised. Was Eve okay? Or was he too late to save her?

Reaching out with his free hand, he pounded his fist on the trunk lid, once, twice.

A resounding thud answered back from against the right rear quarter panel.

"Hang on, Eve!"

The scuffle of gravel in the driveway drew his attention to where Sheriff Adams and his deputy ran toward the situation with their weapons drawn.

"We saw everything, Ryker. Did you hit her?"

"Yeah, got her in the right shoulder, but I haven't seen her move. She's got Eve Brooks in the trunk."

"I'll take point," Sheriff Adams said, easing around the driver's side of the vehicle. He pulled the door open. "Out of the car, Edith, hands where I can see 'em."

"He shot me, Sheriff."

"If he hadn't, I would have. Now out of the car!"

Edith staggered out of her vehicle, blood spreading across the front of her blouse.

Sheriff Adams led her over onto the grass, where he handcuffed her and made her sit down. He took the hand-held radio off his belt and contacted dispatch for an ambulance.

J.P. reached inside the vehicle and pressed the trunk

release. He beat it back around to the rear of the vehicle before the lid had time to fully open.

Eve blinked against the glare of sunlight that pierced her eyes through the open trunk. Then J.P. was there, lifting her out of her tomb and placing her on her feet.

She choked back a sob as he reached down and stripped the tape off her mouth in one quick motion.

"O…uch!" Her skin stung.

"Sorry. Are you okay?"

He turned her and untied the scarf binding her wrists together. She wanted to put her arms around him before she collapsed to kiss the ground under her feet.

"She killed her own nephew, J.P. She would have killed me, too." Turning to him, she slid her arms around his waist and leaned into him. He reciprocated and pulled her close.

"I never should have left you alone."

"You didn't know. Neither did I, and she works for me."

"Miss Brooks?" Sheriff Adams left Deputy Richards to guard Edith Weber and walked over to where she and J.P. stood next to the rear of the car.

"Do you need medical attention?"

"No. I think I'm all right except for a cut on my ribs."

"I've radioed for an ambulance. They'll take a look at you."

"Okay." Eve glanced into the trunk, the claustrophobic cubical that could have been her tomb. "Do you see that?" She motioned to a small shipping box and a large envelope tucked in the well of the spare tire.

"Damn," he whispered as he leaned into the trunk and retrieved the box containing the cut-up rat carcass and the envelope with the ransom note inside. The one they now knew Grimes had constructed.

"Edith never mailed these. They've been in here the whole time."

"She knew who'd sent them, and she couldn't risk having any evidence on them come to light." Eve sucked in a breath and tried to relax, but her nerves were a tangle of knots.

"Tell me what happened."

"She Tasered me upstairs in the lodge and tied me up. She was bent on collecting the ransom money after she'd listened to the real kidnapper's call. She's the one who concocted the scheme. She was the mastermind. She claimed Grimes was nervous about things and planned to go to the sheriff. She killed him to keep him from talking."

"You said she Tasered you?"

"Twice. She has it in her purse."

Sheriff Adams went around to the driver's side and came back with Edith's purse. He closed the trunk and plopped the purse down, unzipped it and fished around, eventually coming up with the Taser.

J.P. put the parcels down and examined the weapon. "The prongs are about an inch apart. It looks like a match to the burns on Roger Grimes's neck, but you'll have to have your forensics department run a comparison to be sure."

The sheriff put the Taser back into Edith's purse, turned and walked back over to where she sat with her head down. "Edith Weber, I'm charging you with attempted kidnapping, extortion, assault and first-degree murder. Deputy Richards, put her in the squad car until EMS arrives."

Edith glanced up, her hatred set in the stony crags of her face as she glared at Eve, before the officer helped her to her feet and led her away.

A shudder wormed its way along Eve's spine and dissipated the second she looked away. A den of snakes had been eradicated, but not without a price. She swallowed against the sense of regret clutching the back of her throat, tipped her head back, rocked up onto her tiptoes and found J.P. Ryker's lips.

"What was that for?" he asked, gazing down into her eyes.

Her breath caught in her lungs, trapped by the feel of his body so close to hers. The things she wanted to do to him and the thoughts associated with the effort launched heat into her cheeks.

"For having the good sense to rescue me before that old bat hauled me away to heaven knows where." Leaning close, she kissed him again.

In the distance she heard the whop-whop-whop of the chopper sweeping into the valley, headed for the landing pad.

"You call for a ride?" J.P. asked, pulling back, but keeping his arms locked around her.

"After you told me about Tyler and I got back to the lodge, I called the hangar and had Henry go and pick up Devon and Tyler's dog, Hank. I couldn't leave them stranded in town."

"That's what I love about you. You're always thinking."

A zing of emotion pulsed in her heart and flooded her brain with the essence of the word. *Love?* Was it possible she could ever experience it again?

"Come on, let's get you cleaned up and checked over. Then I'll head out and let Devon know how much has changed around here in the last couple of days."

J.P. STARED OUT THE window of the chopper as the bird lifted off for their quick trip into the airport in Cascade, where Eve's private jet was waiting to fly them to LAX.

Taking in the view as the ground pulled away, he realized how much he cared about the ranch. Or was it the woman sitting next to him? There was little chance the feeling would be mutual when he finally told her the truth about Shelly. He would do it tonight, as soon as they settled back into the city.

"Are you ready for this?" he asked, glancing over at her. The scarf she'd abandoned for the pressure dressings was now gently draped across the covered scars on the left side of her face.

Concern wrapped around his thoughts. Would she revert to the shattered woman he'd worked so hard to put back together? Or hold on to the transformation he'd witnessed with his own eyes?

"It had to happen sometime. I have to go back and take care of my business." She smiled for him, but he saw apprehension in the set of her perfect mouth, in the ripple of tension playing along her jaw.

Taking a final look at the Bridal Falls Ranch before the chopper gained altitude and crested the mountaintop, he turned his concern to L.A. and the nagging knowledge they were about to trade a set of resolved circumstances for a set that wasn't.

He'd asked plenty of questions in the past couple of days, enough to know neither Tyler Spangler, Edith Weber nor Roger Grimes had set foot out of the great state of Idaho in the past two years.

It backed up Edith's claim that she'd seized on the opportunity the kidnapper's call had presented. Additional searches had proved that none of them owned a voice-modification device like the one used to make the phone calls.

Tension locked down his system. Eve's tormenter was in L.A., of that he was certain.

Chapter Fifteen

"I keep a permanent two-bedroom suite at the Omni downtown for those times I don't feel like battling bumper-to-bumper traffic on the Pacific Coast Highway out to Malibu."

"Nice." J.P. only half heard her. He was too busy tracking the movements of the sleek black car that had been tailing them since they left LAX in the stretch limo.

Traffic on the 110 freeway was light for a Friday afternoon, and the driver was having trouble keeping his distance.

"I want you to look back, see if you recognize the black car in the next lane over, four lengths back."

Eve turned in her seat and stared through the tinted rear window. "No. Looks like everything else."

He had to agree. He was being paranoid. Since they'd landed an hour ago, he'd been analyzing everything that moved for its threat value.

"Relax. Your senses are in overdrive with all the noise and visual stimulation. Happens to me every time I reenter this rat race. Takes a few hours to wear off."

"You seem pretty calm."

"I'm a good faker. I'd rather be curled up on the porch swing back at the ranch right now, sippin' a glass of Charleen's lemonade."

He looked at her, taken by the way she seemed to blend in with the luxurious interior of the limousine as well as she blended in with the simple cushions on the porch swing at the ranch.

But where did her heart lie?

"What time's the meeting on Monday?"

"One o'clock, but my lawyers will be there at noon with a cease-and-desist order for Thomas and anyone he has hired in the last six months. Our legal agreement regarding EBBC will be vacated by a judge on Monday. I'm going to give Thomas a generous severance package and he'll be gone for good."

He didn't know much about how the corporate world operated, and he didn't care to learn right now. His only concern was keeping Eve safe until the threat to her life was extinguished.

"Tell me about your suite at the Omni."

"It's great. I don't have to make my bed, and they put a little chocolate on my pillow every night at turndown." She looked over at him and grinned. "If you insist on knowing, I use a private elevator with a security code to my floor. No one without the magic number gets in. I had them change it a week ago when I knew we'd be heading back to L.A. for the meeting."

"Like I said, always thinking, but once this meeting is over, I want to open my own investigation into Thomas Avery's kidnapping. You're vulnerable until whoever was behind it is caught or killed."

"Does that mean you'll stay on?"

A knot the size of an asteroid orbited in his gut. "For as long as I can." Hell, after he told her the truth tonight, he'd probably be forced to leave. Head back to his office and nurse the crater he'd find in his heart. But what about her? He couldn't risk her life by leaving her alone. Maybe he'd have to call in a favor and spot her with a bodyguard, but the idea of anyone else but him protecting her irritated like ground glass in an open cut.

"We'll get to the suite, unpack, then take my car out and find someplace great for dinner."

He nodded and settled back against the seat, his attention focused on the side mirror, trained on the car tailing them.

L.A. was a new game. He'd have to learn the rules in her world.

Eve adjusted her scarf, pulling it tight across the left side of her face, then double-checked the coverage in her compact mirror. Satisfied, she slipped the mirror back into her purse, pulled out her dark glasses and put them on.

"You might want to brace yourself, J.P."

"For what?"

"I'm pretty certain there's a mole inside the Omni who knows and relays my comings and goings to the tabloid vermin."

He stared at her, seemingly less than interested. "Call an exterminator."

She laughed, glad his sense of humor was intact.

"You remember how chaotic it was getting the calves into the holding pen and separated from their mamas?"

"Yeah."

"It might be like that when we get to the hotel."

J.P. sat up straighter in his seat. A blade of concern sliced across his nerves. "Paparazzi?"

"Yes. Hordes of the little vultures."

"You shouldn't insult vultures like that."

She grinned. "I want you to be prepared to have cameras shoved in your face. You're about to become the subject of tabloid news, if you can call it news. The headlines will probably claim I've been held in an alien space ship for the last seven months and just escaped with the alien sidekick who broke me out."

Now it was his turn to chuckle. "Only if I can be a cow-boy alien sidekick."

He watched her sober, saw the humor drain from around her mouth, saw the slightest tremble of her hands as she worked the handles of her purse, trying to keep her nerves at bay.

He could relate the moment the limo made the turn into the hotel entrance and rolled to a stop under the portico.

A swarm of paparazzi five deep and eight wide had collected at the entrance to the hotel.

Caution sliced through him. "This isn't safe, Eve. What if he's mixed in with them, waiting to strike in all the commotion?"

"Then someone will get a great shot."

"I'm serious."

"So am I. Just sit tight. Hotel security is on the way. They'll hold them back and clear us a path into the lobby."

He didn't like it. Didn't like the fact the situation could spin out of control in a single heartbeat.

Eve reached out and took his hand. "Just promise me you won't let go, no matter what."

"Not a chance." He interlocked his fingers with hers and watched three security guards push through the crowd. Reaching into his shirt pocket, he took out his shades and slipped them on. "Ready when you are."

EVE STEPPED OUT OF THE elevator next to J.P. and spotted her red BMW at the far end of the VIP parking garage. She'd have to turn it over to the valet when they returned from dinner. She just couldn't walk very far in high heels anymore. Heck, she'd give her eyeteeth for a pair of cow-boy boots right now.

Reaching out, she looped her arm in J.P.'s, enjoying his body heat as it warmed her skin, and the slant of the Stetson on his head. He hadn't had much to say since they'd survived their encounter with the rabid pack of paparazzi and checked out the suite, but she was beginning to worry.

Granted, her lifestyle in Los Angeles was extravagant, maybe even a bit overwhelming, but she'd give it all away for a lifetime of days with him at her side.

Somewhere between West 4th Street and South Olive, she'd realized how much she loved him.

"What would you prefer, French or Italian? Patina is on Grand, so is Bottega Louie. It's early. We can probably snag a table without a long—"

He pulled her to a stop and grasped her upper arms. His eyes were bright, charged with blue fire that frightened her. Staring up at him, she felt the slightest vibration in his fingers where he held her. His throat moved when he swallowed. He swallowed again, like a man drowning and searching for air at the same time.

Fear skimmed across her nerves, leaving a hollow sensation in the pit of her stomach. She sucked in a breath.

"I have to tell you something, Eve. Something I should have disclosed a long—"

The deafening screech of tires echoed against the concrete ceiling of the parking structure.

"Run!" J.P. grabbed Eve's hand, catching a streak of black in his left peripheral as the car bore down on them from out of nowhere.

They zagged to the right.

The vehicle passed within a hair's breadth. He recognized the same sleek black car he'd seen following them on the freeway, but it was minus its license plate now.

Brake lights flared red. The driver flipped a 180-degree turn. Smoke spun off the tires as the maniac behind the wheel stomped on the gas pedal and shot forward for another pass.

Squeezing Eve's hand as tight as he could, he aimed for the concrete pillar five yards in front of them.

They had to take cover or be cut down like grass in the open terrain of the parking garage.

Eve's left ankle turned in her shoe. Pain fired into her foot. A scream lodged in her vocal cords.

The misstep brought her to her knees. She lost her grip on J.P.'s hand and skidded forward onto her belly.

Glancing up, she saw the car closing in.

Panic shut down her response. Frozen in place, she felt J.P.'s hand on her arm as he dragged her in next to him behind the concrete barrier.

The car shot past and ran over her high heel. It popped out behind the speeding vehicle and landed with a clop on the concrete.

J.P. pulled his weapon from its holster inside his jacket and raised the Glock, taking aim.

"Don't shoot," Eve yelled. "It's the paparazzi."

Taillights flared for an instant. The car came to a broadside stop.

Caution worked through him as he prepared for another drive-by assault, determined to stop the car with bullets if necessary.

The rear window inched down and a lens snaked out the opening for an instant, then pulled back. The driver hit the gas and the car sped off, then zipped down the exit ramp.

"The bastard almost hit you for a camera angle! Are you okay?" He holstered his weapon, reached down and helped Eve to her feet.

"Better my Manolo Blahnik than my head, and it might have been if you hadn't grabbed me when you did."

"Are they always this aggressive?"

"Sometimes worse."

"Let's have a look at your ankle."

Eve leaned against the cement pillar and pulled up her pant leg.

J.P. knelt in front of her and guided her foot onto his leg, where he could get a better look.

Heat invaded his body as he felt both sides of her slender ankle, noting a patch of bruising along the right side of her foot. "We better get some ice on this to keep the swelling down."

"I'm sure it'll be fine." She lifted her foot off his thigh and set it on the ground.

He rose to his feet and offered her his hand, but she refused his offer with a shake of her head. "No, no. I've got this."

Leaning forward she put weight on it as she lifted her right foot and pulled off her other high heel.

"I think I can walk. We can still go out to dinner." She took a step forward, then another; he caught her on the third step a half second after her ankle buckled under her.

Scooping her up in his arms, he headed for the executive elevator and safety. He wanted her out of the garage now, in case the maniac returned for a freeze-frame.

"Give it a rest, Eve. We're going to ice it and order room service tonight. With any luck you'll be on your feet by morning."

Eve flung the shoe in her hand over J.P.'s right shoulder. It flopped across the concrete floor and landed next to its mate. "C'est la vie, Manolo Blahnik," she whispered as she relaxed against him.

Now they were a pair.

J.P. CLOSED HIS EYES, letting the steaming trail of hot water alleviate the agitation cooped up in his body. He'd been a couple of words away from making a confession to Eve. The fact his reprieve had come from a crazy driver with a high-end Canon didn't sit well. The longer he kept the information to himself, the harder it was going to be once he told her the truth.

He sucked in a breath, taking the steam-laced air deep into his lungs and holding it for a long time before he exhaled.

Bending forward, he hung his head under the steady stream of hot water and tried to come up with a plan he could live with, but every angle formed a sharp edge that stabbed at his heart.

He didn't want to live without her, not a day, an hour, a minute....

A whisper of sound brought his head up.

Slicking the water from his face, he stared through the glass shower door at the foggy confines of the five-star bathroom.

His breath hung in his throat. His body went rigid then melted in the fire of need as he watched Eve step toward him, loosen the belt on her robe and pull it open. An apparition spawned in the backwaters of his mind.

She let the robe slide off her shoulders. It fell to the marble floor, setting off tiny swirls in the mist.

A groan squeezed from his throat, and his mouth went Sahara dry. Staring, he took in every sexy curve of her perfect body. The jut of her round breasts peaked with taut pink nipples. The indent of her slender waist before it swept out to the sensual swell of her hips.

She stepped forward, reached out, opened the shower door and stepped inside, pulling it closed behind her.

Then her hands were on his skin, her fingers exploring the contours of his chest.

He found her mouth and breathed her in. There was nothing unreal about the woman in his arms, nothing superficial or premeditated.

Hunger burned through his apprehension, turning it to sexual need so intense he thought he'd explode. He smoothed his hands over her backside, slicking them over her wet skin. Her entire body quaked under his touch.

Cupping her bottom, he picked her up. She spread her legs and wrapped them around him as he centered her on his hips and backed her into the wall. A sigh puffed from between her lips. Burying himself inside her was what he wanted right now, but he stopped short of satisfying the need. He wanted to indulge hers. Blazing a trail of kisses across the top of her shoulder, he thought of the morning on the swing. The day he'd kissed the scars on her face, the day she'd let him.

He would leave no doubt in her mind tonight that she was beautiful to him.

EVE SNUGGLED INTO HER pillow and gazed over at J.P. He'd made love to her with an intensity that took her breath away, but not before he'd loved her in the most meticulous detail. There wasn't a single spot he'd missed, but she'd done some exploring of her own.

Heat burned her cheeks. Every image of his virile body and their intimate connection was forever seared into her memory.

She closed her eyes in case he opened his and found her watching him sleep.

In the morning she'd tell him how she felt, right after she coaxed him to finish what he'd been trying to say to her before they were interrupted by the paparazzi driver who'd killed her high heel.

J.P. STARED OUT THE WINDOW onto the city below and waited for Eve to dress and come out of the bedroom. It was seven a.m., but a bone-deep ache had awakened him hours ago. An ache he knew would never heal as long as he was alive.

He wanted Eve Brooks. Hell, probably had from the moment he set eyes on her.

"Mmm. There you are." She wrapped her arms around him from behind and put her cheek against his back.

Closing his eyes, he clasped her fingers with his own and memorized the sensation. He'd taken the liberty of contacting an ex-FBI buddy this morning, who'd agreed to act as a bodyguard for her. There wasn't much more he could do, except tell her the truth.

Sobering, he turned out of her grasp. "Eve. Sit down. I have something to tell you."

She smiled, her blue eyes flashing with a sex-crazed glint he found infectious, but he couldn't join in this morning. Couldn't let himself fall under the influence, or he was a goner.

"I've got something to tell you, too," she said. "But you go first, since I'm assuming it's the same thing you were trying to tell me in the parking garage yesterday evening."

"Yeah." He watched her settle on the sofa, but he couldn't bring himself to sit. His nerves were fried, his emotions shot full of holes. The only thing not fazed by this dilemma was his revved-up libido.

He smoothed a hand over his head and stared at her sitting on the sofa in her cowboy boots and jeans.

"You know I worked for the FBI before I opened my security company."

"I did know that."

"What I never told you was I worked the hostage rescue unit as its tactical commander."

"That's a great title. I'm sure you did a kick-butt job."

Frustration jolted through him as he moved closer to

her and perched on the edge of the club chair directly across from her.

"You don't understand, Eve. I worked your half sister Shelly's kidnapping case. I was calling the shots on the ground."

A brief mask of realization slipped across her features and settled in the hard set of her mouth. "You were there that day?"

"I gave the order to move in early on the kidnapper's location. We had it pegged based on a phone trace, but they must have spotted us before we could reach them—"

"Shelly's dead because of you!" Eve's heart shattered into a million tiny pieces. "Because you jumped the gun!"

She stared at the man she loved, the man who'd brought her back to life and sealed it last night in her bed.

The faceless FBI bureaucrat she'd always blamed for her half sister's death was sitting across from her right now, and she'd had the misfortune to fall for him?

Irony branded itself on her soul, sucking the breath from her lungs. She fought off the first wave of a panic attack.

"Go! I never want to see you again." She pushed to her feet, walked to the door and pulled it open.

"Eve, let me explain. I have to—"

"Just go!" She closed her eyes when he hesitated in front of her for a heartbeat, then stepped past. She couldn't risk even a single glance into his eyes, or she'd fall apart before he reached the elevator.

Mustering every ounce of calm she could find, she closed the door softly behind him and crumpled to the floor.

"SCREWDRIVER, ON THE ROCKS, hold the vodka." J.P. slid his empty cocktail glass across to the bartender and slapped a twenty-dollar bill on the bar next to the tabloid rag. He stared at the front-page picture of himself and Eve in the parking garage yesterday. A photo he could use to identify the maniac who'd taken it…if the rag would reveal its source.

He gritted his teeth to keep from mentally strangling the paparazzi jerk who'd taken the shot via distraction on four wheels. The absurd headline was even more outrageous.

Eve Brooks Back from the Brink of Death? What's Wrong with Her Face and Who's Her Cowboy Hunk?

"It's nine a.m., buddy. I'm trying to put together a booze order. You know you can get O.J. over in the Grand Café?"

"I like your orange juice better." And the fact that he could keep an eye on the executive elevator from here. He glanced at his watch. It had been two hours since he'd ripped out his own heart and left it beating on the floor of Eve's suite.

Maybe he should have kept the information to himself.

Maybe he wanted to be able to live with himself.

Maybe he should have told her how she made his heart hammer, and his mouth go dry, and his tongue say goofy things.

Maybe he should have told her he loved her.

"You okay?" the bartender asked as he slid another glass of orange juice toward him on a bar napkin. "You don't look so good."

"I should have said those three words to her face." He picked up the glass and took a sip.

"One-night stand?" The bartender wrinkled up his face.

"I love you."

"That's heavy."

"I know."

He had to go back up there.

"Keep the change." He slid off the stool and aimed for the elevator. She would probably slam the door in his face, but he couldn't let her go without telling her how he felt. Last night had only made it clear.

Pulling the pass key out of his shirt pocket, he put it in the card slot and pulled it out. The doors slid open. He stepped inside and punched in the floor code.

The double layer of security gave him a measure of trust, knowing she was locked safely inside her room. Dear God, he hoped she hadn't experienced a relapse. She'd come so far emotionally from the shattered woman who'd spoken to him from behind the screen, afraid to let him or the world see her face, no thanks to the paparazzi.

The bell in the elevator car chimed, Eve's floor number lit up and the doors eased open.

He stepped out into the corridor. Four doors lined the wall, all private suites like hers.

An odd smell hung in the air, a medicinal odor he associated with a hospital. Had to be something the housekeeping staff used. Strange he didn't see a cleaning cart in the hallway.

Pausing outside the door to her suite, he raised his hand and knocked a couple of times.

"Eve. I know you're in there. I need to speak to you… just hear me out and I'll leave." He waited.

"Eve?" Leaning close to the door, he pressed his ear to the panel. No sound of movement inside.

Caution raked across his nerves, along with the strong chemical scent, stronger now that he was right outside her door.

Sucking in a nose full of the odd smell, he sniffed it out, tracing it to the door handle.

Someone had used it recently with the chemical on their hands.

An uneasy sensation coursed through his body. He dug

in his shirt pocket, took out the room key and shoved it in the slot.

The lock disengaged. He forced the handle down with his elbow to ensure he didn't disturb any fingerprints that might still be on the surface.

J.P. shoved the door open and burst into the room.

"Eve!" Stopping in his tracks, he stared at the trashed room, where a struggle had taken place. A struggle she'd had to endure while he cooled his heels in the bar downstairs.

He reached into his jacket pocket, pulled out his cell phone and dialed 911.

A minute later he was on the line to hotel security.

Chapter Sixteen

J.P. stared out the window, listening to the uniforms speculate in the background. If he could rewind the clock two hours, he'd have stayed with her. His lapse in duty had cost him the woman he loved, but it could cost Eve her life if they didn't find her in time.

"We've got blood."

He turned around and stepped toward the forensics technician holding up a swab tipped in pink where the two-part chemical test had reacted to the hemoglobin in the sample.

"Where did you take it from?"

"What's left of the champagne bottle. Looks like it was used in the confrontation."

Mentally he retraced the scene in his mind. Eve had let someone in. There wasn't any sign of forced entry. Was it someone she knew? Or someone with an access key?

The club chair he'd landed on just before she asked him to leave had been tipped over, maybe when its occupant was attacked from the front. A standing floor lamp beside it had also been knocked over in the struggle.

He knelt down, spotting a dark smudge on the rubbed-bronze fixture. "Take a look at this." He motioned to the technician. "Could be more blood."

"Kind of looks like it. Hard to tell for sure because of

the dark finish." The technician opened another swab and rubbed it across the stain. A drop of phenolphthalein reagent, followed by a drop of hydrogen peroxide, rapidly turned the tip pink.

"Positive for blood."

Pushing to his feet, he stepped back, putting together the rest of the scenario. Eve had probably been sitting on the sofa when the kidnapper entered, or she let him in. The champagne bottle had been his first weapon of opportunity. She must have fought back, and when it didn't bring her down, he'd been forced to use the lamp. But what about the chemical smell? The technician had determined it was ether. He'd probably used it to make sure she was out.

Gritting his teeth, he tried to put the mind-numbing images out of his head, but he couldn't. He wouldn't rest until he found her. He had to get moving.

"Just a heads-up." He gestured to the technician. "You're going to find my DNA in here. I spent the night with Eve Brooks last night."

"Good to know. I'll need an exemplar sample from you to run a comparison."

"Can you take it now?"

"Yeah."

He followed the technician over to the wet bar, where he took a cheek swab from inside his mouth. The man sealed it inside its sterile container. "Name?"

"J.P. Ryker." He watched him label the sample and put it back inside his kit.

"Ryker?"

He turned at the familiar sound of his former FBI cohort's voice. The only fellow agent he'd confided in about his reasons for leaving the bureau.

Mike Bennett extended his hand. "How the hell are you?"

Reaching out, he shook it, noting Mike hadn't changed much in the two years since he'd left the bureau.

"I'll be better when we find her."

"Eve Brooks is your client?"

"Has been for close to a month."

Mike eyed him, speculation drawing his brows together. "Any idea who'd want to kidnap her?"

"The same nut job who kidnapped her business partner, Thomas Avery, eight months ago and wasn't able to collect the ransom."

"I don't think we caught that case."

"I know you didn't. Eve's got a thing against the bureau, seeing how I botched her half sister Shelly McGinnis's kidnapping case three years ago and she wound up dead."

"Simon McGinnis's daughter?"

"Yeah. He's married to Eve's mother, Katherine."

Realization dawned across Mike's features in a mix of surprise and disgust. "Damn. Does she know who you are?"

"She does now. I told her this morning before she was abducted. She was angry. She asked me to leave. I complied."

"You can't blame yourself for this, or what happened three years ago. There isn't an agent on the team that day who wasn't affected by the tragedy."

"I've got to find her, Mike. I'm headed down to hotel security right now to view the hallway security footage."

"You've gotta keep me informed of what you find if you want to stay in the official loop."

"I will." He nodded to his old friend and left the suite. It helped he'd picked up an ally, but the clock was still ticking on Eve's life.

He'd already wasted three hours.

THIRST, BONE-DRY DEATH.

"Wat…er." The word traveled up her throat and rasped out of her mouth. She opened her eyes in the darkness, sensing more than seeing someone in the room. The silence around her was deafening. The hum in her eardrums constant.

Where was she?

She was alive. She knew that much by the excruciating pain circumventing her wrists tied above her head. There was no feeling in her hands, and the chill of the hard floor under her butt confirmed she was sitting on the ground.

The click of a button directly in front of her knifed a beam of light into her eyes.

Mind-numbing pain pulsed inside her head. She shut her lids against the onslaught.

"Drink." The demand was firm and in a female voice.

The maid who'd come into her suite shortly after she'd demanded J.P. leave?

J.P.

The woman clutched her chin, tipped her face up and shoved a water bottle between her teeth.

She swallowed the liquid as fast as she could, but the gusher coming out of the bottle overwhelmed her.

The woman jerked the bottle away.

Fighting to breathe, she choked and coughed until her insides ached.

A wave of nausea roiled in her stomach, but she contained it by sucking air in through her nose and exhaling out of her mouth.

"It's the drug on an empty stomach. I'll bring you something to eat."

Horror skimmed across her fractured equilibrium. She watched the light source on the woman's head gyrate and spin off into the darkness.

She'd been given a drug? It explained why everything was a blur. Everything but her memories of J.P. holding her, loving her. Mentally she hung on to the image in her head and used it to blot out the pain.

I'm here, J.P.... Where are you...?

J.P. RUBBED HIS NECK and rocked his head back and forth to relieve the tension.

An hour and he still hadn't caught a glimpse of anyone entering the suite.

Pressing the advance button, he watched frame after frame of the empty corridor click by.

"Bingo." Taking his finger off the forward button, he reversed the digital video, then hit Play again.

A maid's cart moved into the lower right-hand corner of the monitor. He watched her knock on the door. The door opened. He caught a brief glimpse of Eve. His heart squeezed in his chest. Remorse locked down tight on his conscience.

The woman in uniform entered the suite. He watched the time pass on the time stamp. One minute.... Two.... Three.... Four.... Five, the door opened, the maid snagged her cleaning cart and maneuvered it into the suite, careful to keep her head down. Careful to avoid looking directly into the security camera he was certain she knew was there.

"Dan." He motioned to the chief of security who'd made it his mission to help out any way he could. The reputation of the Omni was at stake. He'd explained he couldn't have guests being kidnapped out of their rooms.

"Did you find something?"

"Yeah. Look at this." He rewound the footage and played it again. "I'm going to need the name and address of that maid."

"Certainly." The security chief went back to his desk and hammered the information into his computer. Two minutes later he handed J.P. a piece of paper with a name, address and phone number.

"According to our payroll department, it's Jenny Garza's floor, but she never clocked in today and she hasn't been to work for the last couple of days even though her cleaning cart is missing. No phone calls either. She's MIA."

J.P. pulled out his cell phone and dialed the number on the paper. It rang and rang, but no one picked up.

"Contact the police, have them do a welfare check at Miss Garza's residence."

Dan nodded and hurried to his desk to call the police.

J.P. rubbed his eyes, praying he could catch a break. Was Jenny Garza involved, or was she a victim of a determined kidnapper who needed her pass keys, cart and floor code to get to Eve?

"It's hot."

Eve forced open her mouth for another spoonful of flavorless soup the woman with the light on her head shoveled between her chapped and swollen lips.

Taking measured swallows, she worked to keep from choking again. Her throat was raw, her sense of place distorted.

"Let me…go," she whispered before the next spoonful appeared in the ring of light aimed at her face. "I'll pay… as much as you want. You can have it all."

Silence. Bone-chilling silence. She shuddered, unable to control a wave of vibration centered deep in her body.

Desperation squeezed her throat shut. She turned her head to avoid the next spoonful of sustenance she was beginning to suspect contained more drugs.

"Suit yourself. It won't be long now."

Eve closed her eyes and sank back into the darkness.

J.P. ROLLED UP ON THE address in East L.A.'s Boyle Heights and parked the courtesy car the hotel had loaned him to drive for as long as he needed it. Dan had relayed the bad news to him.

Jenny Garza was dead.

A knot lodged in his chest and refused to dissolve. If the kidnapper was responsible for the murder of an innocent hotel maid in order to obtain her pass keys and floor codes, what was he capable of doing to his sweet Eve?

He climbed out of the car, spotting Mike Bennett standing inside the perimeter of bright yellow crime scene tape the cops had used to cordon off the single-family home.

"Ryker." Mike saw him and broke out of the circle of agents he was briefing. "Hey, good call, buddy. Unfortunately we're too late."

"You pulled this from the locals?"

"Yeah, we took jurisdiction in the investigation. I'm hoping we can find some evidence to put us on the trail of Eve's kidnapper."

"Did you find Garza's pass keys?"

"Negative."

"What more do you need? Whoever took Eve used the keys they stole from Garza, and the floor code they probably had to squeeze out of her. Any indication she was coerced?"

"Plenty. She was tied to a chair. She has multiple contusions and choke marks on her neck. Someone wanted information and obviously got it so they could gain access to Miss Brooks."

"Any idea what Garza's cause of death is?"

"No. We'll have to wait until the autopsy."

He gritted his teeth. "Better make it fast. Eve doesn't have much time."

"There's something else you need to know. I got a call an hour ago from Thomas Avery, Eve's fiancé—"

"Ex-fiancé."

"Not according to him."

Anger leached from his bones as he stared at Mike and tried to control his emotions. A hothead response wasn't going to do anybody any good, least of all the woman he loved.

"Avery says a call came into his office this afternoon with a ransom demand for Eve Brooks's return."

"Let me quote it verbatim. Half a million dollars in unmarked bills. Put it in a stainless steel briefcase. Not a duffel bag. Wait for my instructions, or she dies."

"I don't know whether to arrest you or try to lure you back to the bureau as a mind reader."

"Same ransom demand that came through in Avery's case and in the contacts the kidnapper made with Eve at her Idaho ranch."

"Avery recorded the call. I've got an agent picking it up right now."

"What's the kidnapper's time frame?"

"Ten a.m. tomorrow."

"Where's the drop scheduled to take place?"

"A storm drain off the Pacific Coast Highway."

The same storm drain where Thomas Avery was held?

"Cross-reference the location with information on Mr. Avery's kidnapping eight months ago. LAPD found him based on directions his kidnapper gave to Eve. Maybe it's the same location the kidnapper has requested for her ransom drop. An area he has scoped out. I'm going to head back to the hotel after I swing by my office and pick up a file."

"You're saying the kidnappings of Thomas Avery and Eve Brooks are linked?"

"Yes. The disgruntled kidnapper contacted her again about a month ago."

"Why would he do that?"

"Because he wasn't able to collect the half-a-million-dollar ransom in the California desert."

At least that's what the kidnapper wanted them to believe.

"Keep me in the loop, Ryker. I'll be back at the Omni in an hour just so you can tell me what the hell's going on."

J.P. nodded and turned for his vehicle, nursing a notion in his gut as fragile as a newborn baby. There was only one way to prove it.

He climbed in the car, fired the engine and pulled away.

If Eve could face down her demons, he could face his, too.

J.P. CLOSED THE BOOTLEGGED file he'd kept locked away in his office for the past three years, a file he'd never read in its entirety, until now. Nitpicky details the follow-up boys in suits had compiled long after tactical storm troopers like him had snuffed out their firepower and gone home. The nitpicky stuff that solved cases, the stuff he'd never appreciated.

Rubbing his hands up and down on his face, he tried to get his mind working again. He closed his eyes for a moment, searching for clarity. Something he could utilize to help find Eve.

The FBI had lifted a solitary fingerprint in the Shelly McGinnis case. A print they'd lifted off her body in the lab using a heated superglue vapor trick. The investigating agents had run the print through IAFIS, the FBI's finger-print identification system, but didn't get a hit at the time.

Would anything pop if they ran it again?

Glancing up, he saw Mike Bennett headed for the make-shift office Dan had set up for him in the hotel's security area, a small cubicle with glass windows down one side, giving him a full view of the entire office space. Reaching down, he slid the manila file folder under the keyboard.

He was a civilian now. Having an open FBI case file in his possession could be considered a crime.

Clicking on the run of security video he'd memorized, he paused and captured the image of the phony maid out-side Eve's suite. A side profile was the best he could come up with. He hit Send and fired the freeze-frame off to the printer.

"J.P." Mike strode into the room and sat down in the chair facing his desk. A frown pinched his forehead. He looked tired and irritable, like a single poke might set him off.

"If you've got something, buddy, you better lay it on me now. She's running out of time."

Mike's comment left a sick uneasiness in the hollow of his heart.

"Three years ago, the suits in the bureau found a single fingerprint in the Shelly McGinnis case."

"I know. I watched the forensics team collect it off of her body in the lab."

"And I know it didn't produce a hit in IAFIS back then, but I'd like you to run it again. Now."

He waded all the way in. "The technician who lifted it indicated it was a small print. He also noted in the file that it could belong to a woman. I've got a woman posing as a maid to gain entry into Eve's suite. If I'm right, we get an ID on her. If not, we keep working."

Mike eyed him for a moment, opened his cell phone and contacted the bureau with his rush request. He hung up and sat back. "This is a stretch, Ryker."

"Is it? I just verified that the ransom demand is the same in all three cases. It's an insignificant amount of money for a family with a combined wealth in the multimillions. Eve's earning the bulk of it through her company, EBBC."

Bennett let go of a whistle from between his teeth. "I see your point."

"Shelly McGinnis's kidnapping was all about the money. An amount the kidnapper saw as significant. The next attempt was aimed at Thomas Avery, and Eve was tapped for the ransom, only the kidnapper wasn't able to collect because a pipe bomb went off next to where Eve was standing, and there was a witness who called the cops."

"That's what happened to her face?"

"Yeah. You didn't read that in the tabloid rag this morning, did you?" A wave of pride surged through him, making him smile as he thought about her courage under fire.

"Eve's ransom request is for the same amount, linking the kidnapper to Shelly, and Thomas, and now Eve."

Mike's cell phone rang. "Yeah. Address?"

J.P. shoved a notepad and pen across to Mike and watched him scribble a name and address on the paper.

Damn, he'd seen that name somewhere before.

Yanking the file out from under the keyboard, he pulled it open and scanned for the woman's name, finding it buried in the interview section.

Mike slapped his phone shut and jumped to his feet. "I'm not even going to ask, Ryker," he said, nodding to the FBI file on the desk. "But we caught a break. The print belongs to a Jacqueline Cordova. It was entered into the database via an employment background check last year.

She works at Hollywood Presbyterian Medical Center and lives nearby. I'm dispatching tactical. Let's go."

"Cordova and McGinnis were enrolled in the same nursing program. The suits interviewed her the day after Shelly went missing." J.P. snagged the phony maid's picture out of the printer as he ran by and beat Mike to the elevator.

He hadn't been able to finish theorizing over the most disturbing aspect of his thought train. The one smothering him with a sense of dread he couldn't shake.

The kidnapper's focus had evolved after Shelly's murder. Their new mark was Eve. But it wasn't about the ransom anymore. It was about something a pipe bomb in the middle of the desert had failed to do.

Kill Eve Brooks.

Chapter Seventeen

"She's pretty out of it."

Eve opened her right eye a crack, just enough to see the woman with the light on her head talking on a cell phone. She'd managed to fake her way out of a dosing in the last round of drug-laced water the woman had tried to pour down her throat by pretending to be unconscious.

"No, I didn't give her too much! I'm not an idiot. I know my Valium. Okay. I'll get started. She'll be wide awake when you get here." She hung up the cell phone.

"Jackass," the woman grumbled as she stepped closer.

Eve slipped back into her sleep act, but almost cried out as her captor cut through the tape she'd used to secure her hands above her head.

Life-giving blood pulsed back into her fingers, tipped with fingernails she wanted to jab into the woman's eyes, but she remained limp, waiting for the right moment to strike.

"Jacqueline Cordova! FBI! Open the door!"

Mike Bennett gave the nod.

J.P. stood on the outskirts of the action and gritted his teeth. As a civilian, he wasn't allowed to play a role in the takedown. If it weren't for Mike Bennett, he'd be sitting in a bureau car a block away.

Thump! Thump! Thump!

A third brutal impact with the battering ram and Jacqueline Cordova's front door caved on its hinges. The mass of wood and splinters slapped back into the wall of the entryway.

"Go! Go! Go!"

One after another, the agents stepped over the threshold and disappeared like ants into a sidewalk crack.

Frustration put J.P. in motion. He sprinted onto the front lawn and took cover behind a eucalyptus tree. Close enough to hear the shouts coming from inside, but the calls weren't what he wanted to hear.

"Clear!"

"Jacobs?"

"Clear!"

"Young?"

"All clear, Bennett."

"Matthews?"

"Clear."

He buckled against the trunk of the tree and closed his eyes. Every cell in his body ached for her. He had to find her. Where in the hell had the kidnapper taken her? The possibilities in a city the size of L.A. were endless. They were running out of time.

"Ryker!" Mike yelled from just inside the door. "Get in here. I think we've got something."

A spark of hope hissed through his veins. Pushing away from the tree, he jogged up the walk, taking the steps two at a time.

"One of my guys found a planning session on the wall in a back bedroom. Eve's at the center."

He pushed through the door and followed Mike down the hallway and through a bedroom door on the right, where a couple of the agents had congregated. They immediately parted when he stepped up to stare at the patch-work scraps of information pinned up with thumbtacks. He swallowed the tension that had him by the windpipe and stared at the eight-by-ten glossy of Eve.

Gritting his teeth, he reached in his jacket pocket and pulled out the picture of the phony maid taken by the surveillance camera at the hotel. He unfolded it and handed it to Mike.

"Have your boys see if they can find a photograph of Jacqueline Cordova in the house. Do a comparison."

"Matthews, take a look." The agent snagged the picture and left the room.

"You care about her, don't you?" Mike asked from next to him.

"What gave it away?"

"The way you looked at her picture just now."

J.P. grinned, ignoring Mike's attempt to quantify the nature of their relationship.

Agent Matthews came back into the bedroom carrying a picture frame containing a photograph of Jacqueline Cordova in a nurse's uniform, her name tag clearly visible. "Looks like her, Chief."

Mike took the two photos and held them out. "J.P.?"

"The chin, the nose, it's her. Cordova took Eve." Turning his attention back around, he studied a blueprint tacked on the wall in front of him. It was marked up in some areas with a yellow highlighter.

Recognition pulled him closer to the line drawing. "I'll be damned."

"What is it?" Mike moved closer.

He traced his finger over the blueprint in search of identifying information and found a tiny set of letters along the bottom right edge.

A cold chill worked his muscles. "It's the Omni, Mike."

"You sure?"

"Yeah." Pinpointing the executive elevator in the hotel lobby, he traced it up to Eve's floor. "Her suite is here. The corridor has been highlighted. It's the route the maid took after she went into the room and incapacitated Eve. I suspect she put her in the cleaning cart so she could get her out without being seen."

With his finger he picked out the highlighted route. "She went to the service elevator, down to the basement and loaded Eve into some sort of vehicle from this area right here." He pointed out a square room off the main corridor that was shaded in.

"Maybe not," Mike said as he studied the drawing. "The service entrance is on the north side of that building. I had my agents check it out. This highlighted area is on the south side."

Tension coursed through his body, twisting his nerves into knots. He stared at the blueprint, trying to make sense of what was right in front of him.

"If this is Cordova's premeditated escape route from the hotel, and we have no reason to believe it isn't, then there aren't any indications that she ever left the hotel with Eve."

"You've been all over the security footage. Did you ever see her leave?"

"No." Alarm ticked through him. "Eve's in the belly of the hotel, right under our feet." He tapped the blueprint with his finger. "She never left. She's right there. I'm going to get her."

SALVATORE FERRAGAMOS?

Eve stared at them in the light someone had turned on in the small gray room. Her throat closed, locking the breath in her lungs as she studied the expensive shoes paired up in front of her.

In increments she paced her gaze all the way up to the man wearing them until she met his cruel stare.

"Did you miss me while you were banging around in the wilds of Idaho?" Thomas Avery asked without taking his eyes off her.

A wave of nausea surged in her stomach. She fought it back with several gulps of oxygen and glanced around the room for anything she could use as a weapon, but came up empty.

"You SOB!"

"I'm sorry it had to come to this, Eve. If you'd have died on the side of the highway that night like you were supposed to, none of this would have been necessary. I'd be sitting on the pile of cash I've embezzled from your company and soaking up the sun on a beach in Brazil."

"You bastard! You planted the pipe bomb that destroyed my face." But it hadn't destroyed her.

"I hired the anarchist who did, and who planted the other pipe bombs to make it look like a random act of violence. But instead, you lived and took off to that damn ranch in Idaho, where I couldn't touch you. Even the phone calls I made to you as the kidnapper didn't get you back here. But threaten your company, and bam, you're here."

Disbelief hitched to her brain as she stared at him. "What now?" Fear climbed over her nerves. "You collect the ransom and disappear, climb back underneath whatever rock you slithered out from?"

He knelt beside her. "I kill you. Leave you to rot down here until someone discovers your body and the cops conclude you were murdered by your kidnapper. Our legally binding employment contract with its gaping loophole in regards to your untimely death will be put permanently in place, and I'll control what's left of the company without your once-beautiful face. I'll declare bankruptcy in a year or two, and walk away." He reached out to stroke his knuckle down her left cheek.

She dodged his touch, pushed back and spit on his hand.

"Bitch!" He wiped it across his pant leg and backhanded her across the cheek before she could react.

Resolve burned through her as she glared at him without flinching.

J.P. had taught her she had courage. Now she knew it was true because she felt it surge in her veins, giving her the strength to stay alive any way she could. Strength to fight the monster she'd once thought she loved. She knew better now. She'd experienced real love. The love of a man she knew would come, but she had to hold on. Had to keep Thomas on the defensive, bide her time.

"There are no loopholes, Thomas. My lawyers were thorough, the best money can buy."

"Stupid little rich girl. My cat's got more claws than you. You failed to include an exit strategy in the event of your death. My lawyers are already preparing to exploit the legalities."

Eve glanced away at the sound of the door and watched it swing open, catching a glimpse of the corridor beyond the solid metal barrier of her prison. Pipes and conduit, the hiss and grind of machinery. She could be anywhere a building existed.

The door slammed shut and she stared at a young woman who stared back, minus the light on her head. The maid who'd entered her suite when she'd answered her knock, then cracked her on the back of the neck with a champagne bottle. But she'd fought back, evidenced by the scrape across the woman's right cheek, until she'd been overpowered and hit with the lamp then had a stinky cloth slammed against her nose and mouth so hard, it split her lip.

"Eve, this is Jackie. My sister."

A scintilla of recognition zipped across her mind. She chased it, trying to run down exactly where she'd seen the woman before. It hit her all at once. A cry raised in her throat.

"I know you. You and Shelly—"

"Amazing," Thomas mocked. "The world is such a small place."

"You were Shelly's friend from nursing school. She brought you home with her over Christmas break one year."

"That's right." She stepped forward, shoved her hand into the pocket of her jacket and pulled out a gun.

Fear twisted along Eve's spine, raising the hair on the back of her neck.

Jackie casually handed the pistol to Thomas.

"Thanks, sis. Did your friend file off the serial number?"

"Just like you asked."

Eve stared up at the two of them, noting their similar features, the coloring they shared. Thomas had claimed he was an only child.

Waves of terror crashed inside her as she put the scenario together. "You two were behind her kidnapping."

"Have brain, will function." Thomas snorted. He stared down at her and shook his head. "Poor Shelly. Nice girl. Too nice. Let her guard down. She was dead ten minutes after we put her in the trunk."

Rage exploded inside her. She lashed out, clawed her way across the floor, aiming for Thomas, oblivious to everything around her except the need to hammer her fists into him for killing Shelly.

Pop!

A single shot bit into the floor next to her, sending chips of concrete flying. It ricocheted into the wall with a thud.

Eve froze.

"The next one's straight at you."

She rocked back onto her butt, feeling her fight wane. "How'd you kill her?"

"Accident. I choked her for too long. By the time we got her back to the flophouse and opened the trunk, she was dead. We made the ransom call anyway, got the hell out of there and dumped her the next morning at her gate."

Tears burned the back of Eve's lids. Tears for Shelly. Tears for the time she'd spent blaming J.P. and his team for getting her killed. Tears for the open wound the kidnapping had left on her and her parents.

J.P. HELD UP HIS BALLED fist and signaled a stop. "You hear that, Mike?"

"Copy. Could have been a gunshot. Came from the left side of the corridor."

J.P. turned on the miniflashlight in his hand and pointed it at the detailed schematic Dan had given them of the sealed-off section of the hotel's basement, set to be renovated in the coming month. Uneasiness furrowed his insides as he studied the map. He wanted to charge down the hallway, guns blazing, and take what was his.

"There are two rooms on the left. One is maintenance storage, the other an antiquated heating and AC control room."

Caution steeled his nerves and dialed his focus down the long narrow corridor. He killed the light and stowed the map.

"Let's move." He didn't wait for Mike, not this time. This time he was going to get to Eve before it was too late.

THOMAS RAISED THE PISTOL, his eyes bright in the overhead fluorescent as he took aim, pointing the barrel at her chest where she sat on the floor.

Eve stared, gauging his actions in milliseconds, waiting for her opportunity to strike. No matter what, she planned to live to tell J.P. he wasn't responsible for Shelly's death. Even if it might be with her dying breath.

Thomas reached up and brushed the side of his hand across his forehead.

Jerking to the left, she raised her leg and jammed her booted foot into his kneecap. The pistol discharged. A bullet whizzed past her ear.

Thomas stumbled back and dropped the gun. It clattered to the ground.

Jackie dove for it at the same time she did.

In a tangle of hands and arms, the weapon skidded free. Thomas scooped it up.

Wham! The metal door kicked back and slapped against the wall.

Thomas spun around, gun raised.

Pop! Pop!

J.P. double-tapped Avery and watched him drop. He stepped through the doorway and kicked the pistol away, into the corner of the room.

"Stay on the ground!" Mike trained his weapon on Jacqueline Cordova and reached for the handcuffs on his belt. Two more members of the tactical team appeared in the doorway.

J.P. holstered the Glock and collapsed on the floor next to Eve. Reaching out, he gathered her in his arms. She shivered as he smoothed back the hair from her face and kissed her forehead. He breathed her in, pulling her tight against him.

"Are you hurt?"

"Not anymore. I knew you would come," she whispered against his neck.

"I never should have left you alone in the suite. I should have stayed to fight."

Pushing back, she stared up at him, her eyes shimmering with tears ready to spill over. "Thomas killed Shelly. He admitted he choked her. She was dead and gone before you ever hit their location, and I owe you an apology." Her voice raised in volume as she looked at the other agents in the room.

"I owe all of you an apology. You did everything you could to save Shelly McGinnis. Thank you."

Exhausted, she leaned back into the comfort of J.P.'s arms and closed her eyes.

"Let's go, sweetheart. Get you checked out and cleaned up." He pushed to his feet and helped her to stand.

"Can you walk?"

"I'm not sure. She fed me a boatload of Valium."

"Jacqueline Cordova," Mike Bennett said as he pulled her to her feet, "you're under arrest for kidnapping and murder. You have the right to remain silent." He handed her off to Agent Matthews, who picked up the Miranda as he escorted her out into the corridor.

Turning his attention to Thomas Avery, Mike felt for a pulse, then shook his head. "Better help her out of here, J.P., before things get crazy. I'll take her statement after things calm down."

"Thanks, buddy. We'll be upstairs."

"Upstairs? You mean that bastard has been holding me hostage in my own hotel?"

"Yeah." Scooping her up in his arms, he headed for the doorway and stepped out into the semidark corridor. "But the good news is it looks like your Monday afternoon meeting has been canceled. Wanna spend it with me?"

"What did you mean back there, when you said you should have stayed to fight?"

Tension wrapped around his nerves. The idea of putting his heart out there was almost as dangerous as facing down a band of armed thugs, but she'd already taken him hostage.

"I was headed back up to the suite." He stopped walking and pressed into the corner at the end of the hallway to let a couple of FBI agents hurry past. "To tell you I love you, Eve, and whether it's requited or not, it doesn't matter."

"You rugged cowboy types are just too perfect to live without, you know that?"

"What?"

She smiled up at him, letting his admission smooth off the jagged edges of her heart.

"I love you back, J.P., and then some."

The air caught in her lungs as he leaned in and gently kissed her face, avoiding her swollen lip, where her scrape with Jacqueline Cordova had left a mark.

"I've got a week's worth of damage control to do at Eve Brooks Bridal Couture and an internal audit to launch into Thomas's embezzlement claim, along with any other malicious acts he instigated. But I'm going to tap some good people inside the company to run the place. And after that—" she smiled up at him "—I want to go home."

His eyes turned smoky blue with sexual heat she wanted to feel on every inch of her body.

"Will you take me back to the Bridal Falls, J.P., and love me forever?"

"Try to stop me, sweetheart."

Epilogue

"I do." Eve mouthed the words as she gazed up into J.P.'s eyes.

"Do you, John Paul Ryker, take Eve Marie Brooks to be your lawfully wedded wife, to love her, honor her, cherish her, and forsaking all others, commit yourself only unto her?"

"I do."

"Then in the presence of God and these witnesses, I now pronounce you husband and wife. You may kiss your bride."

J.P. fingered Eve's veil and raised it to expose every inch of her beautiful face. Gone were the dressings and scarves forever. She'd given *Elle* magazine an exclusive interview along with pictures, and in return she'd received overwhelming support and acceptance.

Hunger burned in the center of his chest for all they'd come to mean to one another since leaving L.A. and the rat race behind.

He found her lips and kissed her solidly on the mouth. Her arms locked around his neck.

Pulling back, he stared down into her eyes and grinned.

"Ready to take the plunge with me?" he asked.

She nodded and smiled back. "It's not as much fun in clothes," she whispered.

"It's my honor," the minister said, "to present to you, Mr. and Mrs. J.P. Ryker."

A round of applause went through the gathering of their parents, family, friends and the ranch crew they'd invited to the base of the falls to share in their happiness.

Eve gazed at J.P. Her heart was so full, she knew she'd burst if he didn't hurry up.

Extending her hand, she gave the minister her bouquet of wildflowers and smiled sweetly. "Will you hang on to these for a moment?"

"Certainly, dear."

On cue, J.P. scooped her up in his arms in a billow of tulle and lace, then stepped up onto the flat rock with her in his arms.

"Are you sure about this?" he asked, grinning at her from under the brim of his new black Stetson.

"Never more than I am right now."

In two steps, they were airborne and diving off into heaven.

* * * * *

COMING NEXT MONTH from Harlequin® Intrigue®
AVAILABLE FEBRUARY 5, 2013

#1401 ULTIMATE COWBOY
Bucking Bronc Lodge
Rita Herron
A tough cowboy determined to find his missing brother... An FBI agent who blames herself for the boy's disappearance... A ruthless criminal they're determined to catch.

#1402 HOSTAGE MIDWIFE
Cassie Miles
Entrusting her life to playboy Nick Spencer, midwife Kelly Evans has one chance to rescue eight hostages, including a newborn, from an office building rigged with explosives.

#1403 PROTECTING THE PREGNANT PRINCESS
Royal Bodyguards
Lisa Childs
A pregnant princess needs protecting, and royal bodyguard Aaron Timmer is just the man for the job. But in order to protect Charlotte Green, Aaron first has to find her.

#1404 GUARDIAN RANGER
Shadow Agents
Cynthia Eden
Veronica Lane knows that Jasper Adams isn't the type of man she should fall for...but the ex-Ranger is the only man who can keep her safe when she's targeted for death.

#1405 THE MARSHAL'S WITNESS
Lena Diaz
When her identity is leaked to the mob, a woman in Witness Protection must go on the run in the Smoky Mountains with her U.S. Marshal protector.

#1406 DANGEROUS MEMORIES
Angi Morgan
A U.S. Marshal vows to protect a witness with repressed memories while solving her parents' murders, discovering what's truly important in life and rekindling their passion.

You can find more information on upcoming Harlequin® titles, free excerpts and more at www.Harlequin.com.

HICNM0113

REQUEST YOUR FREE BOOKS!
2 FREE NOVELS PLUS 2 FREE GIFTS!

HARLEQUIN®

INTRIGUE®

BREATHTAKING ROMANTIC SUSPENSE

YES! Please send me 2 FREE Harlequin Intrigue® novels and my 2 FREE gifts (gifts are worth about $10). After receiving them, if I don't wish to receive any more books, I can return the shipping statement marked "cancel." If I don't cancel, I will receive 6 brand-new novels every month and be billed just $4.49 per book in the U.S. or $5.24 per book in Canada. That's a savings of at least 14% off the cover price! It's quite a bargain! Shipping and handling is just 50¢ per book in the U.S. and 75¢ per book in Canada.* I understand that accepting the 2 free books and gifts places me under no obligation to buy anything. I can always return a shipment and cancel at any time. Even if I never buy another book, the two free books and gifts are mine to keep forever.

182/382 HDN FVQV

Name	(PLEASE PRINT)
Address	Apt. #
City	State/Prov.	Zip/Postal Code

Signature (if under 18, a parent or guardian must sign)

Mail to the **Harlequin® Reader Service:**
IN U.S.A.: P.O. Box 1867, Buffalo, NY 14240-1867
IN CANADA: P.O. Box 609, Fort Erie, Ontario L2A 5X3

**Are you a subscriber to Harlequin Intrigue books
and want to receive the larger-print edition?
Call 1-800-873-8635 or visit www.ReaderService.com.**

* Terms and prices subject to change without notice. Prices do not include applicable taxes. Sales tax applicable in N.Y. Canadian residents will be charged applicable taxes. Offer not valid in Quebec. This offer is limited to one order per household. Not valid for current subscribers to Harlequin Intrigue books. All orders subject to credit approval. Credit or debit balances in a customer's account(s) may be offset by any other outstanding balance owed by or to the customer. Please allow 4 to 6 weeks for delivery. Offer available while quantities last.

Your Privacy—The Harlequin® Reader Service is committed to protecting your privacy. Our Privacy Policy is available online at www.ReaderService.com or upon request from the Harlequin Reader Service.

We make a portion of our mailing list available to reputable third parties that offer products we believe may interest you. If you prefer that we not exchange your name with third parties, or if you wish to clarify or modify your communication preferences, please visit us at www.ReaderService.com/consumerchoice or write to us at Harlequin Reader Service Preference Service, P.O. Box 9062, Buffalo, NY 14269. Include your complete name and address.

HI13

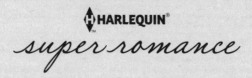

"How *did* you find me, Eva? I'm not exactly listed in any phone books."

She rested her suddenly shaky hands on her knees. "Someone told me you might be able to help me, so I decided to track you down. I'm…well, let's just say I'm very skilled when it comes to computers."

His jaw tensed.

"You're good, too," she added with grudging appreciation. "You left so many false trails it made me dizzy. But you slipped up in Costa Rica, and it led me here."

Tate let out a soft whistle. "I'm impressed. Very impressed, actually." He made a tsking sound. "You went to a lot of trouble to find me. Maybe it's time you tell me why."

"I told you—I need your help."

He raised one large hand and rubbed the razor-sharp stubble coating his strong chin.

A tiny thrill shot through her as she watched the oddly seductive gesture and imagined how it would feel to have those calloused fingers stroking her own skin, but that thrill promptly fizzled when she realized her thoughts had drifted off course again. What was it about this man that made her so darn aware of his masculinity?

She shook her head, hoping to clear her foggy brain, and met Tate's expectant expression. "Your help," she repeated.

"Oh really?" he drawled. "My help to do what?"

God, could she do this? How did one even begin to approach something like—

"For Chrissake, sweetheart, spit it out. I don't have all night."

She swallowed. Twice.

He started to push back his chair. "Screw it. I don't have time for—"

"I want you to kill Hector Cruz," she blurted out.

Will Eva's secret be the ultimate unraveling of their fragile trust? Or will an overwhelming desire do them both in? Find out what happens next in SOLDIER UNDER SIEGE

Available February 2013 only from Harlequin Romantic Suspense wherever books are sold.